MINIONS OF THE MOON

Alias the Night Wind

BY VARICK VANARDY

The Blue Fire Pearl: The Complete Adventures
of Singapore Sammy, Volume 1

BY GEORGE F. WORTS

Clovelly

BY MAX BRAND

Drink We Deep

BY ARTHUR LEO ZAGAT

The Gun-Brand

BY JAMES B. HENDRYX

Jan of the Jungle

BY OTIS ADELBERT KLINE

The Moon Pool & The Conquest of the Moon Pool

BY ABRAHAM MERRITT

Tarzan and the Jewels of Opar

BY EDGAR RICE BURROUGHS

War Lord of Many Swordsmen:
The Adventures of Norcross, Volume 1

BY W. WIRT

MINIONS OF THE MOON

WILLIAM GRAY BEYER

INTRODUCTION BY

SAM MOSKOWITZ

COVER BY

RUDOLPH BELARSKI

ALTUS PRESS
2017

© 2017 Steeger Properties, LLC, under license to Altus Press • First Edition—2017

EDITED AND DESIGNED BY
Matthew Moring

PUBLISHING HISTORY
"Minions of the Moon" originally appeared in the April 22 & 29, and May 6, 1939 issues of *Argosy* magazine (Vol. 289, No. 6–Vol. 290, No. 2). Copyright © 1939 by The Frank A. Munsey Company. Copyright renewed © 1966 and assigned to Steeger Properties, LLC. All rights reserved.
"Let 'Em Eat Space" originally appeared in the November 4, 1939 issue of *Argosy* magazine (Vol. 294, No. 4). Copyright © 1939 by The Frank A. Munsey Company. Copyright renewed © 1966 and assigned to Steeger Properties, LLC. All rights reserved.

THANKS TO
Gerd Pircher

ISBN
978-1-61827-305-5

Visit *altuspress.com* for more books like this.
Printed in the United States of America.

TABLE OF CONTENTS

INTRODUCTION

SAM MOSKOWITZ

LONG BEFORE THERE were science fiction magazines, the one consistent source for those "hooked" on such tales was the great weekly adventure pulp, *Argosy*. Not only was *Argosy* receptive to good science fiction, but its editors actively searched out and encouraged writers who could do a professional job in this specialized field. When we speak of *Argosy* we must also include its memorable companion *All-Story Magazine,* with which it combined in 1920.

A few of the popular authors they introduced to science fiction and fantasy were Edgar Rice Burroughs, A. Merritt, Ray Cummings, Murray Leinster, Erle Stanley Gardner and many others.

After the science fiction magazines were established, *Argosy's* new additions were generally recruited from these sources and its own protégés became less frequent. An interesting exception was William Gray Beyer. Little information is known concerning him, the publisher of his only book "Minions of the Moon" (Gnome Press, 1950) is able to reveal only that he had been a Philadelphia policeman. *Argosy* serialized "Minions of the Moon" in three installments beginning in its April 22, 1939 number where it scored an instantaneous hit. Beyer had a light, breezy style that carried the reader easily along. His characterization of a disembodied intelligence, "Omega" in that story proved a tantalizing memorable one.

Later, reader and editorial demand produced a series of

sequels, all of short novel length: "Minions of Mars," "Minions of Mercury" and finally "Minions of the Shadow." For a while it appeared that a new reader's favorite had come into being. However, when *Argosy* was sold by Munsey to Popular, Beyer no longer appeared and except for a single short story and a brief revival when his first novel, "Minion of the Moon" was published in book form and later reprinted in *Two Complete Science Adventure Novels Magazine* in 1952, he disappeared from the fantasy scene.

MINIONS OF THE MOON

*Mark Nevin was a healthy young man whose
appendix, of all prosaic things, led him into
unbelievable adventure. For, Mark's doctor had
perfected a tremendously powerful anaesthetic,
and after sleeping peacefully for twenty-
two days, Mark slipped quietly into a state of
suspended animation. He didn't wake up until
the Year A.D. X2, and the first thing he did was
to make friends with the Man on the Moon and
Miss America of the Day After Tomorrow.*

CHAPTER I

THE UNKNOWN YEARS

THERE SEEMED TO be no rhyme or reason to anything, Mark reflected sleepily. In the first place, no such healthy specimen as he had any business with an inflamed vermiform appendix. And certainly there was no sense in old "Chisel-chin," the physician, making him sign a bunch of papers giving authority to administer his new anaesthetic. He could have used it without asking permission, and nobody would have been the wiser. He hadn't asked the consent of the guinea pig he had tried it on in the lab.

Mark chuckled, half awake. It seemed to have worked, he decided, for here he was coming out of it, *sans* pain—which meant *sans* appendix.

Something was wrong however, he mused, almost rousing himself to the task of lifting his eyelids. One thing that bothered him was a strong musty odor, one of the few not usually found in a hospital. Another annoyance was the hardness of his bed. He was almost convinced that he had been placed in some dungeon under the hospital, after the operation. Fine way to treat a paying guest!

A sudden and confirming drop of water splashed on his forehead, snapping him completely awake. Somebody would hear about this, he vowed, opening his eyes. An impenetrable blackness was the reward of this effort.

Attempting to rise, he received a jarring thump on the head and fell back. With a surge of panic he realized he was in a coffin! A questing hand had encountered nothing but hard, cold stone on all sides. His own breath, condensing on the lid of the coffin, had caused the drop of water!

Buried alive! He fought to calm himself. The whole thing was probably a dream anyway—a result of the anaesthetic. People had such dreams when under the influence of ether. And besides, they didn't use stone coffins any more....

It *had* to be a dream. Yet why was he so lucid, and why did he feel that trickle of water advancing, inch by inch, down the side of his face? Sensations were never so clear in dreams.

And how long had he lain there, assuming this were not all a figment of the imagination?

Abruptly he stirred, pressing his elbows against the sides of the coffin. A swirling cloud of dust choked him. The cloth of his shroud had disintegrated, giving rise to the musty odor and the dust which he had disturbed. Centuries must have passed since the operation!

With a burst of frenzy he pressed upward against the lid of his coffin. Quite unexpectedly it raised. A full foot of it extended past the hinges, effectively counterbalancing its great weight. He sat up.

A LARGE, domed, stone vault met his surprised gaze. Two small windows admitted cheerful beams of sunlight. He shielded his eyes, stung by the sudden transition from complete darkness.

Cautiously he climbed from the coffin, half fearful that his legs would crack or collapse under a weight they had not borne for many years. He was surprised and relieved to find that after stretching he seemed as well and strong as before the appendix trouble. A hasty examination disclosed that the incision had healed nicely and left but the thinnest of scars.

And here was a strange situation, Mark decided. Instead of being alive and well, he should be quite defunct. It was only logical to expect his body to be in the same deplorable state as the grave clothes which fell in dust as he moved. His eyes

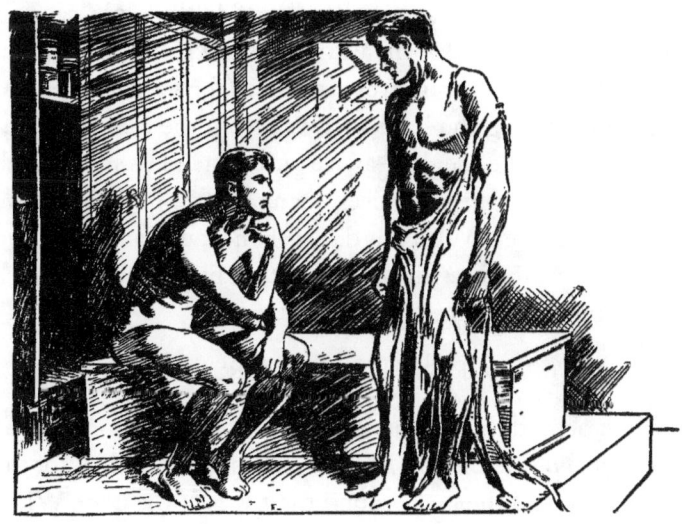

"Look here," Mark said, his graveclothes dangling about
him. "You can't use that body. It's exactly like mine!"

chanced upon the hinged top of the coffin. Whoever had designed that counterbalanced lid had evidently expected it to be
lifted from the inside. Most irregular indeed.

A more thorough inspection of his surroundings revealed
several additional irregularities. The vault, he noticed, looked
more like a locker room than a tomb. Its walls were lined with
shiny, stainless-steel cabinets, the doors of which were sealed
with wax. There were so many of these that the only bare spaces
were those occupied by the two small, paneless windows and a
door.

On impulse he strode toward the latter with the idea of
seeing what the world looked like outside. He caught himself
up short, however, when he saw his reflection in one of the
shiny surfaces flanking the door.

"That will never do," he said aloud. "There just might be
someone around who objects to nudism. Maybe I had better
explore those lockers. Should be some clothes inside if my guess
is right."

The sound reverberated hollowly inside the vault, causing him to shiver in spite of the warm breeze which was entering one of the windows. His eyes cast about for some implement with which to dig the hardened wax from the cabinet doors. He found what he sought—an ice pick of stainless steel, which would serve the purpose, nicely-hanging from a hook above one of the cabinets. With this discovery he found another thing he hadn't seen before. The compartment beneath the ice pick was inscribed with the legend:

OPEN THIS ONE FIRST.

Mark obeyed the instructions without delay. Removing the wax turned out to be simple. Long strips of it rifted out of the cracks as he slid the pick around the edges of the door. When the last chunk had been pried loose, he stepped aside as he tugged on the door handle. The precaution was the result of a last-minute thought that he might be greeted by a cloud of the same kind of musty dust that he had stirred up in the coffin. Obviously time had passed—lots of it—since he had been placed in this tomb, and any ordinary fabrics in the cabinet might well be in the same condition as his grave raiment.

HIS APPREHENSIONS proved to be groundless, however, for the cabinet contained a phonograph and a large rack full of records. Mark noticed that a record was already on the playing disk so he wound the machine and started it spinning. The welcome voice of old "Chisel-chin" with its nasal twang, blared forth from the horn:

"At the present time, which is twenty-two years after the administration of the drug which placed you in a state of suspended animation, there is no discernible change in your body. The flesh is soft, the blood fluid; and X-ray photographs show all internal organs to be in perfect condition. Following the operation you remained unconscious for more than two weeks— quite sufficient time for the incision to heal—before gradually falling into the state of suspended animation in which your body now lies.

"It is my belief that you may awaken some day, although every attempt of mine to bring you to life has failed. When this may occur there is no way of guessing. A hundred years may pass, or even a thousand. It is with this thought in mind that I have spent the last few years in preparing a resting place for your body which will survive the ravages of time, and stocking it with supplies which will enable you to live under any adverse conditions which may prevail.

"I say this because in recent years the world has gone from one devastating conflict to another, and with no end in sight. There is every possibility that you will awaken to find a world of barbarism, in which mankind has fallen to a low state. This is only a guess, but I have provided you with weapons of the latest design with which to defend yourself.

"There are also hunting rifles using cartridges of small caliber, but far higher in velocity than any in existence in your time. Your marksmanship will render these small bullets as effective as larger ones in the hands of a less experienced person.

"Knowing this, I chose weapons of light caliber because of the smaller space needed to store a large quantity of ammunition. In the cabinets on the far wall, is enough to last a lifetime. It is interchangeable in side-arms and rifles except in the case of the tiny hand-machine-gun you will find. This weapon is to be used at close quarters—less than a hundred feet—and fires slugs smaller in size than the needle in this phonograph. They barely penetrate the skin at full range, but a person hit by one drops instantly. The tips of the needles are coated with a poison which causes instant coma, lasting several hours. Be careful how you handle them.

"There are several cabinets filled with clothing of all kinds, made of the spun-glass fabric which has become popular in recent years. This cloth is durable and not apt to disintegrate with time, being of inorganic origin. Other compartments will reveal a supply of preserved foods in glass jars, quantities of distilled water—just in case you aren't able to find natural water in the vicinity—and tools and implements of varied uses. The records in the rack may furnish you amusement, if you find yourself bored.

"In stocking this vault, I have included everything a man might need to survive in a hostile environment. It is my sincere hope that the nations of the world will settle their difficulties and you will awake in a world of peace and progress, but from present indications it would seem that such is not to be. These cabinets you see about you are an old man's best efforts to atone for a great wrong.

"Goodbye and good luck, my boy."

FOR A long minute, Mark allowed the record to spin, after the voice had ceased, then bestirred himself to turn off the machine.

"You did a good job, doc," he said, addressing the phonograph. "But you forgot to mention just where the heck this tomb is situated. But I guess it doesn't matter. I'll see for myself."

Picking up the ice pick he started to chip away the wax which sealed the next cabinet. He was beginning to get thirsty and hoped to uncover some of the distilled water mentioned by the doctor. The task was barely started when a voice suddenly shouted in his ear: "North America!"

Mark instinctively ducked and whirled to face the speaker. No one was there! He leaned weakly against the cabinet, bathed in cold perspiration, and wondered if his long sleep had affected his brain. Then, when there was no repetition of the astral voice, he resumed his chipping, muttering aloud. Abruptly he was interrupted again.

"Stop mumbling, my fine-feathered corpse!" the voice scolded. " 'Tis not seeming. And besides, it's a nasty way to treat a guest. If I were you I wouldn't let my eyes pop out like that. Somebody might step on them."

Mark, by this time firmly convinced of his own insanity, decided to humor himself.

"No self-respecting corpse would entertain an unattached voice in the privacy of his own tomb," he stated, returning to his task. "You must bring your body when calling. It is one of the first rules of etiquette."

"The nerve of the cub!" the voice complained, talking to itself. "And me an old man when his ancestors were hanging by their tails. All right, you perambulating cadaver, here's a body for you."

CHAPTER II

IF A BODY MEET A BODY

MARK RESIGNEDLY TURNED around to see what new trick his senses were going to play on him. There, balanced on one foot atop the coffin lid arms outstretched, in a pose that might have done credit to an aesthetic dancer—a slightly cracked one—was a well-muscled masculine figure, gazing with a silly expression at the ceiling. Mark walked around the apparition and examined it critically. No, really; this was going too far.

"Look here. That won't do," he said firmly. "You'll have to get another. That's mine you're wearing now."

The figure floated gently down, seated itself on the edge of the coffin, and assumed the attitude of Rodin's *Thinker*.

"You humans are the most specialized sort of beings I've ever encountered," he marveled. "I've been studying your race since early Grecian times, and I've never seen two exactly alike. For instance, I remember a man who used to write poetry in a Scotch dialect, and he bemoaned the fact that a person never could see himself as others saw him. And here I give you the opportunity to do that very thing, and you complain."

"Nobody ever saw me in a pose like the one you were just

in. You're what I would call a phony facsimile. You look like me, but you don't act like me. Say, don't you have a body of your own?"

"Alas, no," the phantom admitted sadly. "I once had a beautiful body, too. Eight legs, three pairs of the most gracefully undulating tentacles you ever saw, and a chitinous armor which was my special pride and joy."

Mark clucked his tongue in sympathy. "Must have broken your heart to part with it, old man. But it seems to me it must have looked like a spider, if you don't mind my saying so."

Mark's facsimile jumped to his feet, and struck a calculatedly bellicose pose. It muttered angrily and glared. "I don't like the way you said that. Take it back?" he challenged. Then suddenly changing his mind, sat down and fell back into the *Thinker* attitude. "As a matter of fact, my race did resemble the arachnids, though we had none of their objectionable habits. Then too, we had six tentacles, far more efficient members than anything owned by a spider—or a man either, for that matter. We could do things a man wouldn't even attempt with his silly hands and their stiff-jointed fingers."

Now it was Mark's turn to be angry. "Don't be absurd. If you ever saw anybody play a piano, you wouldn't talk about stiff fingers. Why, I've seen—oh, I don't know why I'm arguing with you. You're only a figment of my imagination. I'm going to find something to drink."

The embodied apparition again leaped to his feet, glaring at Mark, who unconcernedly resumed his wax-chipping. Ignored, Mark II began pacing in circles around the coffin and muttering to himself.

"What a vanity," he fumed. "Me, a figment of his imagination. It's more likely *he's* a figment of my imagination. I'm crazier than he is. Always have been." He stopped to address Mark the first in a patiently instructive tone. "You're digging at the wrong door if you want water. That one is full of preserved fruit. The next cabinet has corn and beans. The one on the far right contains water. So if you think I'm an hallucination, see if I'm not right."

Mark looked at his replica in astonishment. "You mean you want me to prove that you're not a mere fragment of a temporarily disordered imagination? But if I do, that means you must be a specter or a ghost, and I won't believe that either."

"I don't care what you believe," Mark said sulkily.

The last of the wax was loosened and he opened the door. Shelf upon shelf covered with jars of preserved fruit met his gaze. Mark was astonished, to say the least, but he contrived to hide it from his visitor by quietly closing the door and starting to work on the door at the extreme right.

"For a mere hallucination," he remarked, chipping away with a great show of nonchalance, "you do seem remarkably accurate in your predictions."

"I notice you're working on the one with the water," Mark said, sarcastically.

AND WATER it was. Mark was not really surprised this time. After finding the fruit he had realized that this nightmarish creature knew what he was talking about. There were too many other things that might have been in that cabinet to attribute the phantom's wisdom to guesswork. The phantom knew; but just how he knew was a mystery yet to be solved.

Mark dug the wax stopper out of a three-gallon bottle and let a quantity of refreshing, but flat-tasting water trickle down his throat. Then with the remainder he washed the clinging dust from his body, while the facsimile looked on with an expression of amusement on his—or rather Mark's—face.

"What are you going to dry yourself with?" he inquired loftily.

Mark looked about him helplessly, then brightened up. "If you will stop showing off and tell me which locker my clothes are in, I'll find something."

"Not necessary," Mark said, reaching out his hand. In it appeared a long, fuzzy, bath towel. Mark controlled an urge to gape, and took the towel.

"Thanks," he said, applying the creation, which seemed to absorb water quite as well as one manufactured in the usual way. "You'll have to teach me that trick sometime. But right now I wish you'd tell me just what you are, and why you insist on haunting me."

The phantom hopped up and down in fury. Most of the time his feet didn't touch the ground, but that didn't seem to bother him, not in the least.

"Insults!" he howled. "Nothing but insults! I'm not a ghost. I refuse to be considered a ghost!"

Then, as if he took perverse pleasure in self-contradiction, his flesh slowly became transparent and finally melted away, leaving nothing but the bony framework, which proceeded to drape itself in the familiar attitude, atop the coffin lid.

"Don't do that," Mark begged. "It's—it's disgusting."

"I shall do it if I like," the skeleton answered, snappishly cracking a fleshless knuckle. "It's cooler."

Mark sighed resignedly and sat down on the far end of the coffin, determined not to be surprised at anything that might happen from now on. He noted with interest that the skeleton had a neatly-healed break in a collar bone. The visitor surely was carrying out the duplication to ghoulish perfection. Mark remembered receiving that break in the last quarter of a college football game during his senior year, and was pleased to see that it had knit so well.

"It's a long, sad story," began the skeleton, in a hollow voice. "My race was born, and lived out its life on the Earth's satellite. It is remarkable, when you think of it, that a race could evolve far enough to reach a high state of development on that little planet. Gravitation being slight, the Moon lost its atmosphere at a fast rate. The entire habitable life of the planet lasted hardly longer than one geological age of the Earth.

"My people advanced rapidly, I suppose, because we worked as a unit. No dissension; no individual ambitions. Every one of us strived for the advancement of the race, not for his own betterment.

"But things happened rapidly on my world. Eventually we had to burrow underground and establish great sealed caverns in which life could continue independently of the fast failing air supply on the surface.

"BUT JUST as my race had evolved rapidly, it declined also at a fast pace. The time came when, out of the vast millions which once roamed the planet, there were only a few dozens of us left; and these few had almost completely lost the power to reproduce.

"I was one of these, in fact one of the last to be born. At an early age I showed signs of being a little—well—" the skeleton smirked modestly—"unique. I saw no sense in co-operating with the others in finding a way to increase our reproductive capacity. It was my contention that a million ordinary people were of no more use than a few high-grade specimens. Quantity was not to be more desired than quality. My aim was to find a way to preserve the lines of the few who remained.

"Nobody agreed with me, of course, so I had to work alone, solving the problem without aid." His tone now became happily martyrish. "I devised a radioactive fluid in which a brain could live, immersed, forever. For several million years, anyway. The body would have to be abandoned, of course. The others finally accepted my idea, inasmuch as they had failed to reach their own goal.

"Unfortunately it didn't work out so well in their cases. They had absolutely no sense of humor. Their lives had always been so serious that when they were freed from the eternal struggle for existence, they were unable to satisfy themselves with abstract thought. The sustaining necessity to solve vital problems had been removed.

"For a time they occupied themselves by inventing imaginary problems, and then joining in finding the solutions. But this was just silly and eventually they began to fall into periodic

stupors, each of longer duration, until finally their brains ceased
to function altogether. At least there has been no thought ra-
diation from any of them for over fifty thousand years."

"They still exist then?" queried Mark.

"Oh yes. They can't die, in a physical sense, as long as they
remain immersed in the fluid. They still lie in their containers
in the interior of the Moon, protected from any possible harm
by a spherical wall of force which we created as a stasis in the
fabric of space shortly after we abandoned our bodies.

"That was the only project that I ever joined the others in
accomplishing. It was a great idea. The whole planet could
disintegrate without harming the brain containers. The stasis
can only be dissolved by the agency which created it—the
combined thought force of many powerful brains!

"I suppose I may as well believe you," Mark sighed. "Here
you are, sitting on my coffin, looking like the breakup of a hard
winter, and your brain really resides on the Moon. But I must
say I wish you'd just quietly passed out the way your pals did,
instead of going about shedding sweetness and light in people's
tombs—particularly mine. I don't suppose I could persuade you
to go away."

THE SKELETON ignored him. "The main point in which I
differed from my contemporaries lay in the fact that I had a
sense of humor," the skeleton went on. "Maybe you've noticed.
I'm a psychological mutant. My mind was never geared to the
eternal struggle for existence, as theirs were. I could never
believe that just living on was of much importance. A race of
beings content to inhabit a small satellite of a minor planet of
a fourth-rate sun, struck me as being pretty small potatoes. To
coin a phrase." The skeleton giggled.

"After we had forsaken our bodies," he went on, "and our
brains had taken up residence inside our wall of force, I couldn't
join the others in their pointless games. I had to have something
to amuse me. So naturally I went exploring. Not physically, of
course. My race had mastered thought long before I was born.

By projecting my ego where I wished, I was able to observe life on the other worlds, some of them far outside the solar system."

"Wait a minute," interrupted Mark. "Am I to understand you are really doing your thinking from the brain on the Moon, and these creations of yours—the body you just had, the awful thing you're wearing now, and the towel—are mere hypnotic suggestions which you have impressed upon my brain by means of projected thought waves?"

"Nothing of the sort," the skeleton snapped, "You couldn't dry yourself with a hypnotic suggestion."

Mark pondered this for a moment. "No," he admitted, "but I could imagine I had, if you hypnotized me into thinking so."

"And catch an imaginary cold, I suppose," remarked the skeleton sarcastically. "You have the wrong idea. I wouldn't hoax anybody into seeing things that don't exist. It's hard enough to believe the things that do exist. That towel is just as real as any matter is. So was the copy of your body, and so is this skeleton.

"Of course matter isn't so very real, at that. Matter is only a function of space. So is energy. Space is the only real thing. Energy—regardless of its form—is merely a wave in space caused by some action of matter. And matter is merely a concentration of space-in-motion, the motion being caused by energy. It's all very simple."

"Yes, of course," agreed Mark. "Only I don't understand it."

"You will when you've lived a few more thousands of years. As for doing my thinking from the Moon, I don't. When I choose to go exploring, my intelligence leaves the brain and travels instantaneously to the place I wish to go. Then, if I want a body, I merely create one from the energy waves which abound in space. But no matter what form of body I may acquire, I always retain the senses and powers with which a free intelligence is endowed."

"How convenient," Mark commented. "But if you can do all this independent of your brain, it wouldn't matter much if your brain were destroyed, would it?"

Rattling nimbly, the skeleton jumped to its feet. Mark winced.

"Gracious me!" the skeleton exclaimed. "I never thought of that. Here I've been jumping in and out of that brain for thousands of years—and never considered that I might not need the pesky thing at all. I'll have to think this over. Goodbye for now!"

CHAPTER III

WELCOME STRANGER

ABRUPTLY THE VOICE ceased and as it did the skeleton collapsed in an untidy heap on the floor. Mark sensed immediately, with a certain feeling of loneliness, that the intelligence had left for parts unknown. The pile of bones proved that the brain's creations were of real matter and only disappeared when he purposely destroyed them.

"Well," Mark thought, "he left me with a set of spare bones, at any rate."

A rush of memories—of people he had known, places that were familiar to him, and things he had held dear—came to trouble him as he found himself alone once more with his thoughts. He was glad now that he had been pretty much alone during that earlier, far-off part of lifetime. There was no wife to mourn, no sweetheart. That would have made it harder. It wouldn't be an easy thing to suddenly realize that a girl—*the* girl whom you had last seen alive and lovely and young was now nothing but a crumble of dust, dead for hundreds, perhaps thousands of years.

Gloomily Mark attacked the wax on another of the cabinet doors. Finishing this one, he went on to the next and the next, trying by means of sheer activity to close his mind to thoughts of a world long dead.

Before he had removed the wax from the last of the doors,

he was wondering in what part of the world his tomb was, and how many centuries had passed since the operation…. "Did I ever tell you about my operation?" he could ask. "Well, it was about four thousand years ago…." A fine thing.

His visitor had hinted that he was still in North America. That was indefinite but he supposed it didn't matter. Everything would be different anyway. The phantom had claimed that Mark would understand the complex nature of space, matter, and energy when he had "lived a few more thousands of years." That might imply that he had already lived a few thousands of years. On the other hand if he were to assume that it did, he must also assume that the specter was speaking seriously and really meant that he had thousands more years to live. Which, of course, was pure rot.

It obviously wouldn't do to put too much faith in anything the creature had said, he decided, inasmuch as it had freely admitted being more or less crazy. "Just a goofy ghost," he tried to tell himself, firmly averting his eyes from that messy pile of ribs, tibia, clavicles, vertebrae and bony etcetera on the floor.

A GLANCE through one of the small windows revealed that the nearby country was heavily wooded and the ground covered with dense underbrush. This decided him on what to wear, and he set about to select it. The first three cabinets he examined contained ordinary street apparel. The old doctor had evidently held out some hope that the old civilization might continue after the wars were over.

But the next five lockers indicated that this hope had been none too strong, for they were stuffed with clothing designed for outdoor life. Two more of the cabinets were filled with underwear and another contained shoes and boots. In a short time Mark was dressed to cope with the surrounding forest, and equipped with weapons to take care of any wild life he might encounter.

In addition to the highly efficient automatic pistol, he carried a stainless-steel hand-axe fastened to his belt. The underbrush would make this a valuable tool. A small pocket compass should prevent getting lost, and the tiny, needle-throwing machine-gun nestling beside it in a jacket pocket might come in handy in dealing with any hostile humans he might meet in his travels.

Mark really didn't expect to find the world greatly changed, but he certainly wasn't taking any chances. For all he knew his period of suspended animation might have lasted only a hundred years or so. It was hard to say just how long it might have taken for his grave-clothes to disintegrate. The clothing he was now wearing showed no signs of age, but then of course he had the doctor's story that they were made of some new fabric of glass, although they certainly didn't look it. As far as the incident of the spook was concerned, he wasn't at all sure now that he hadn't dreamed up the whole upsetting incident. He fervently prayed that it was so.

Considering everything he decided it wouldn't be at all unlikely that he would find a civilized community a few hours' walk from the vault.

The doctor's fear that the wars going on at the time of his record, would leave the world devastated and civilization wrecked, were very likely exaggerated. He had heard the same fears expressed many times before, and nothing of the kind had happened.

As a last preparation before venturing forth he took a long swig from the bottle of insipid water. He had no intention of returning to the tomb until he had done some extensive exploring in the neighborhood, and there might not be any streams handy. As he returned the bottle to the cabinet his eyes passed fleetingly over the compartments containing the food supplies. He wondered if he shouldn't eat something before he left, but decided he wasn't particularly hungry.

The forest was an impenetrable tangle of trees in all stages of growth. Mark noticed that the underbrush wasn't nearly as thick as he had supposed. The window, he remembered, had shown him only a small view and in that direction there were several dense clumps of foliage.

He was about to replace the hand-axe when he changed his mind and tucked it back in its belt-strap. It would be worth carrying for use as a trail marker.

The sun, although he couldn't see it through the tall trees, seemed to be southeasterly, which indicated that it was before noon. This left him plenty of time to explore before dark drove him to shelter. Without any particular reason, for one direction is as good as another when you have no idea where you are, he decided to follow Mr. Greeley's advice.

A FEW hundred years ago—or was it a few thousand—Mark had possessed a unique propensity for getting into trouble. His small inheritance had made it possible for him to get along comfortably without any sort of salary. And he had found it impossible to live a routine existence. Athletics had provided a suitable outlet for the surplus energy; but he has also been cursed with an overwhelming curiosity concerning almost everything on earth. As a consequence he had often poked his handsome nose into places where people displayed alarming readiness to bash it flat. This instinct had apparently survived the years of suspended animation, for westward was the one way he could have chosen that would lead him into trouble in practically unlimited amounts.

This fact was not to come to light until Mark had covered quite a few miles. Indeed it seemed as he trudged along in the forest that never in his conscious lifetime had he encountered a more peaceful portion of the earth.

Sunlight filtered, here and there, through the dense, leafy canopy overhead and made bright patches on the ground, lending cheer to the grayish twilight which pervaded the lower reaches of this vast woodland. The songs of unseen birds among the branches, and the occasional squirrel who sat back on its haunches to gaze in frank curiosity, only to dart suddenly up the bole of a tree at his approach, combined to lull Mark into a dreamy—and utterly misguided—sense of security.

So rapt was he in his lyrical contemplation of nature's beauty that he went on blissfully for quite a distance before he remembered that he had completely neglected to mark the trees to indicate his trail.

He stopped, half minded to retrace his steps, when it occurred to him that he had been walking in a straight line since the last mark, and it should be easy to bridge the gap on his return. To make sure, he marked several trees close together in a line in the same direction, then continued on, satisfied. The precaution was entirely useless. But he didn't find that out for quite a while. In fact if he could have foreseen what lay ahead, it is likely that even Mark would have locked himself in the tomb and refused to budge a step.

Merrily whistling a tune which had enjoyed tiresome popularity at the time of his operation, Mark's springy tread carried him momentarily closer to disaster in one of its milder forms.

He was wondering if it might not be a good idea to climb one of the higher trees and get a bird's-eye view of the surrounding country. For all he knew his path might lead him endlessly through the woods, while a short distance to the right or left might lie the edge of the forest. He was on the point of climbing a likely looking tree when he was startled by a raucous yell and the sudden appearance of a score of half-naked, black-bearded men. Most of them were brandishing crude spears, but some of them were armed with knobby clubs.

With a draw which would have done credit to Wild Bill Hickok, Mark snapped his pistol into action.

The nearest of the attackers let fly with his spear just as the automatic left its holster. Mark dodged and fired. The savage collapsed like a puppet when the strings are dropped. But in the next instant Mark was felled by a club which struck him behind the knees. Firing wildly, he hit two others before being pinned helpless beneath the weight of a half-dozen vile-smell-ing bodies. He struggled for a moment, but he stopped when he found he wasn't getting anywhere.

THE LEADER, an unkempt hulk of a man, placed the point of his stone-tipped spear at Mark's throat and jabbered to the others to release him and form a circle about him. Lying flat, with the spear-point teasing his Adam's apple, and a dozen more aimed in his general direction, Mark decided that he was outnumbered. The savages evidently didn't intend to kill him, or they certainly would have done it by this time. That being the case, he might as well wait for a more auspicious moment to get away. The little gun in his pocket, with its load of several hundred poisoned needles, would take care of this nicely—if they failed to search him.

When the leader saw that his captive was going to be philosophic about the matter, he withdrew his weapon and motioned Mark to get up. The pack drew closer to inspect the specimen they had bagged, but the leader growled something and they stepped back, muttering in protest.

A series of moans and groans from a point outside the circle gave evidence that one of the victims of the pistol was still alive, but the savages paid no heed to their disabled comrade.

The leader's eye was caught by the shiny, stainless steel axe, and he yanked it from its strap, hefted it, and placed it in the band at the top of the short skirtlike garment which was his only attire.

Mark submitted with the mental reservation that when the time came he would take it back with interest—in the form of a piece of the thief's hide.

The gun had disappeared. Mark remembered it had been knocked from his hand when the pack had jumped him, but it didn't seem to be anywhere in sight now. He supposed one of his attackers had purloined it before the chief had had a chance to see it. He piously hoped the unwashed devil would shoot himself with it.

The leader grunted a series of commands to his crew and

they prepared to march off through the forest in a direction to the left of Mark's former course. Mark gave a relieved sigh as he realized that they weren't going to search him, and his tiny gun was safe.

He decided that his captors were unfamiliar with any wearing apparel more complicated than the crude loincloths they wore themselves. It was unlikely that they would think of the possibility that clothes might conceal weapons.

Two of the savages walked behind him, prodding his spine with their spears; while the rest of them gathered in front and on either side.

The leader looked at the two motionless figures of the men killed by Mark's bullets, saw they were dead, and turned to the wounded man. The man stopped his groaning and looked up with eyes filled with a sort of fearful pleading. The leader prodded him with a foot and grunted a command. The wounded one lifted a hand and answered in a whine. The chiefs next act was to skewer the man neatly with his spear. He roughly withdrew it and ordered the party on its way, ignoring the final thrashings of the victim of his cold brutality.

CHAPTER IV

THE LADY IN THE CAGE

SEETHING INWARDLY, BUT unable to do anything about it, Mark trudged along to the accompaniment of an occasional prod from the spearmen behind him. They seemed to be having a lot of good, innocent fun, but fortunately their spear-tips were not very sharp and the jabs were seldom delivered with sufficient force to pierce the skin. Mark gave no sign that he so much as felt them—he remembered his James Fennimore Cooper and the savage's reputed admiration for stoicism—but this failed to deter the torturers in the least.

They were evidently carrying on just for their own amusement and didn't seem to care how Mark felt about it, one way or the other. As a matter of fact, the pain wasn't so great and after a while he found it possible to ignore it completely and think of other things.

There was, of course, the language to consider. What he had heard of it seemed to consist of a series of guttural, grunting sounds, wholly unlike anything in his experience. Certainly it was not any dialect of English, Spanish or French.

Of course there were some pretty primitive Indian tongues, but these lads were certainly not Indians, even if they obviously were savages. They were altogether too hairy. They looked more like gorillas, he noticed, except that a gorilla wasn't so ugly.

No, they certainly weren't Indians; so they must be some kind of reverted white men; and their language, therefore, must be the degenerate remnant of some white man's tongue. Possibly even English.

This was disheartening, since it plainly indicated that he had been in the tomb for a lot more than a mere hundred years or so. And if one group of humans had chased themselves back to the Stone Age, all mankind might very well be at the same level. Little Mark, he thought glumly, and His Time Machine. Little Mark and The Shape, for Pete's sake, of Things to Come....

Their weapons, he saw, were even more primitive than those of the most backward peoples of his own time. Stone-tipped spears and rough-hewn clubs. No metal—not even bows and arrows. The Australian bushmen had been better equipped. They at least had the boomerang, which was a pretty scientific instrument; and they were accepted as the most primitive of the earth's dwellers. Well, it seemed they had lost their claim to distinction. Meet the new champs.

This thought, and a few others that suddenly popped into his head, provided him with something that in a sufficiently murky atmosphere might pass for a purpose in life. This was how he looked at it. First: that at the end of any war or other catastrophe which might disrupt civilization, certain groups—aggregating millions of people, perhaps—would survive, separated from each other by distances not easily spanned, due to failure of ordinary means of transportation and communication. These groups would be faced with a flock of problems incident to continued survival. Some sort of government would be needed; food supplies must be provided, and clothing and housing against the inevitable approach of winter.

Each group would have so many things to do—things of immediate importance to its own continued existence—that no time could be wasted trying to contact the others. Another deterrent to communication would be the fact that in each community the leader, or clique of leaders, would be too jealous of the power gained to risk it by inviting overtures from other groups. This had happened after the fall of the Roman Empire and had very likely, happened again.

Each of these groups would thrive in a manner dependent upon the facilities at its disposal, the leadership available and the type of people to compose it. These factors would vary to a great degree in different groups, and in some cases civilization would not lose much, while in others retrogression would take place immediately and speedily. Mark was of the opinion that he had fallen into the hands of one of the latter, one which had slipped about as far as man could slip.

His hope was that somewhere there was a people who retained the culture which this bunch had lost, and he intended to start searching for them as soon as he made his escape.

The second thought that cheered him was that even if the first thought was wrong and the world was completely populated with people like the ones he was mixed up with now, he would at least have a lot of fun looking for the other kind, even if they didn't exist. For Mark had always found the hunt more exciting than the kill.

THEY EVENTUALLY emerged from the forest and started across a broad plain. The destination of his captors was now in sight, a mile or two from the edge of the wood. Here lay a scattered group of mud huts, baking in the heat of the midday sun. There were about a hundred of them, a disordered cluster of decidedly unwholesome appearance.

Mark decided immediately that his visit was going to be of very short duration. As they drew closer, a vagrant breeze carried to them a tasty bouquet of decayed garbage and close-packed humanity.

The proddings of the two at Mark's back became more insistent, and he obligingly increased his pace. The whole pack seemed anxious to arrive home as soon as possible to show him off. A clamor arose from the huddle of dwellings—Mark could not bring himself to think of them as houses—and a straggling crowd hurried to meet the conquering heroes. From that point on, Mark's escort closed its ranks, completely blocking him. They seemed suddenly intent on shielding him from the curious gaze of the horde.

At least that is the way he interpreted their action, and he didn't like it a bit. Not that he particularly wished to be admired, but when one considers that his captors had probably not had one bath between them in all their odorous lives, it is understandable that he preferred them not to crowd so close. As a matter of fact, he had guessed wrongly as to the meaning of their maneuver. They were merely protecting him from the exuberant spirits of the good villagers, who probably would have torn every piece of clothing from him and perhaps a bit of flesh as well.

In a few minutes Mark found himself thrust through the gate of a circular enclosure of ten-foot pikes, set a few inches apart, and secured from further separation by strands of tough vines. The gate was slammed shut and fastened by a simple latch which he could have opened by simply reaching hand through the pikes, except that a guard was stationed to see that he didn't.

For a few minutes the hut-dwellers fought with the guard to open the gate and get in, but seeing that he had the situation well in hand they eventually desisted. This conclusion wasn't reached, however, until several victims of the guard's club lay unconscious on the ground. Paying no attention to these casualties, the crowd proceeded to relieve its high spirits by throwing garbage, stones and clods of dirt at the captive.

They soon tired, however, for the pikes were set too close together to make this sport worthwhile. A good proportion of the stones thrown bounced back and hit others in the crowd, which started a few minor riots, much to Mark's savage delight. Mark was really surprised at the amount of venom these brutes uncovered in him.

He gave so much attention to the crowd that it wasn't until it had quieted down that he noticed there was another tiny enclosure, similar to his own, just a few paces to the left.

His audience was milling about so much that it was some time before he was able to see whether or not it was occupied. None of the quaint villagers were molesting the other corral and for that reason he supposed it was empty. Of course, it might also be that the enclosure had an occupant who had been there for so long that he had lost popular appeal. His fickle public had deserted him in favor of a newer attraction—Mark— who was thinking he should have been in vaudeville.

FINALLY THE crowd parted and he obtained an unobstructed view of the other pen. For a second he caught his breath, speechless. There was an occupant, all right, and it wasn't a man. His fellow prisoner, as far as he could see through the close-set pikes, was a woman, and a decidedly lovely one at that.

It might be mentioned at this point that Mark had never been anything that could be thought of as a ladies' man. And since his last brush with a member of the opposite sex, in the course of which he had been both annoyed and thoroughly disillusioned, he had been exceptionally wary and distrustful of all womankind. So when he saw this lovely creature regarding him steadily with one clear, brown eye—the other being behind a pike—there was a long, breathless instant in which he could do no more than stare dumbly back at her. It was during this endless instant that one of the fun-loving citizens managed to toss a clod of earth through the bars with commendable aim. The missile landed athwart Mark's nearer ear, sprinkling clumps of dirt inside his shirt.

"Lovely people," he finally remarked, wondering if the vision would grunt in reply. He wanted to tell her swiftly not to reply. Gibberish from those lips would have been sacrilege.

"Yes, aren't they?" she returned, in accents clear and unmistakably English. "You should feel honored. They've deserted me completely."

"Oh!" blurted Mark, "I didn't expect you to speak English."

The lady straightened up, indignantly. "You didn't think I might be one of those?" She inquired haughtily.

Mark glanced confusedly at some of the unclad slatterns who made up a good proportion of the crowd which was now listening open-mouthed to the conversation of the prisoners.

"No, no," he hastened to assure her. "It's just that I've been asleep for a few thousand years, and I didn't think the language had survived that long."

She looked at him quizzically for a minute before replying. "You have been asleep for a few thousand years," she repeated. "How interesting. I hope I'm not intruding."

With this observation the young lady turned her back and gazed absorbedly through the opposite side of her prison. She quite evidently regarded Mark as being an unmitigated liar slightly on the boorish side. Ordinarily Mark would have been glad to see the end of the conversation, even on that basis, but this time he chose to deceive himself with the thought that here was his only chance to learn something about this new world, and therefore he must convince her that he was all right.

"Please forget I said that," he begged. "It's perfectly true but we'll drop it if it bothers you. I hope I'm not stealing your thunder."

She turned around. "You certainly are," she said. "Although

when I was captured this morning, most of the creatures were out in the fields. But those who were home managed to make quite a turnout. Look at me, would you?"

MARK WOULD, gladly. The girl's clothing covered slightly less than one-fifth of her well-formed anatomy, and consisted mainly of an abbreviated pair of shorts, and something eye-fillingly narrow that seemed to be a cross between a shirt and a brassiere. It covered her shoulders and had sleeves three inches in length which made it resemble a coat—but it fell justifiably short of concealing the lower ribs. The material was satinlike.

Mark gaped as the girl showed him those portions of her skin which had been bruised, soiled, and otherwise damaged by the missiles of the savages. His best offering in sympathy was a dry clucking of his tongue.

"Of course," the girl remarked, "these brutes probably do that to make their victims more tender."

"Tender?"

"Yes. I suppose they will give you another treatment. You will probably be too tough to suit them."

Mark was silent for a minute trying to figure out this last. "I'm a bit dense," he admitted, "but do I gather that these people intend to eat us?"

The girl looked surprised. "Of course," she answered. "Didn't you know? They always eat captives. It's part of their charm."

Mark suddenly felt weak in the knees. This was more than he had bargained for. Something would have to be done, he decided, and groped for the needle-gun inside his jacket pocket.

"You don't seem very concerned," he observed.

"Oh, but I am," she insisted. "I'm so scared I'm beginning to jell."

"You don't look it," Mark accused.

"Naturally not. From childhood my people are trained to be stoical. You see, it frequently happens that one of us gets captured by these wandering tribes. And that nearly always means torture. A person who shows no fear or pain gives very little entertainment for the torturers. So they soon get tired and kill him, which is a boon for the captive."

"You aren't very fussy about boons, are you? Wouldn't it be a lot more sense to build a wall around your city and thus prevent these captures?"

"Our city has a wall," she returned. "But our farm and pasture lands are too big to go inside it. And the cannibals are too clever to attack an armed body of our citizens. They always pounce on just one or two and make off before a rescue can be attempted."

CHAPTER V

DINNER AT FOUR

MARK WAS AWARE that as they talked the mob of savages gradually lost interest and drifted away. There were now only a few remaining. He suddenly realized that no more likely moment to escape was apt to turn up. His guard was absently scratching himself sleepily and watching two boys engaged in a wrestling match. The other guard was, just as sleepily, contemplating the beauties of his prisoner.

This effrontery, Mark decided, entitled him to be the first to sample a few of the needles. He put the idea promptly into action. He fired. The guard stiffened, looked startled, and crumpled to the ground. The girl, without so much as batting an eye, reached a hand through the pikes to unfasten the latch, while Mark turned and treated his own guard to a short burst from the gun.

This one stiffened also, but declined to fall. Instead he looked reproachfully at his attacker and calmly unlatched the gate.

"To think," he said sadly, "that after all I've done for you, You'd try to shoot me. Shame on you!"

"The Goofy Ghost!" Marked exclaimed, and the guard looked

more reproachful than ever. He didn't like to be considered supernatural.

Mark noticed that the girl was having trouble opening the gate against the dead weight of the fallen guard. As he went to help her the erstwhile apparition strode in front of him, calmly picked up the obstruction and tossed it, without effort, through the side of the nearest house. With a loud crash the flimsy, baked-clay wall fell to pieces, preceding the other wall and the roof by only an instant.

"Now you've done it," Mark groaned. "That'll raise the whole colony. Let's get out of here!"

His prediction came true before the noise of the collapsing dwelling had died out. Already men were running from the nearer huts, and the two boys who had been enemies only a moment before were now united in screaming and pointing toward them as they fled.

WITH GLEEFUL strokes the phantom plied his club in a sincere determined effort to decapitate as many of the towns-men as possible. Any that managed to escape his gleeful swings were taken care of by the needlegun in Mark's steady hand.

The girl ran nimbly between them.

Of all the spears which were hastily thrown at them, only two registered hits. One of these was tossed at pointblank range toward the phantom's borrowed body. It shattered itself on his club and a moment later the thrower fell before that same club. The other spear, however, entered the phantom's back and stayed there, swinging to and fro, unheeded. Mark noted this fact idly, thinking it scarcely worthy of comment.

Once a burly figure rounded one of the dwellings and leaped directly in their path. He was no more than a yard away when he appeared. Mark's pulse gave a jump as he caught the flash of his own axe descending toward his head! In a split second, he discarded the thought of using the needle gun. No drug could act quickly enough to stop that streak of razor-keen steel. With a quick sidestep to the right, he put all his weight into a crushing left uppercut. The axe dropped as its wielder fell unconscious. Mark retrieved it, recovered his stride just in time to direct a stream of needles into another of the brutes.

The edge of the settlement was reached without further mishap, and they continued trotting toward the forest. Occasionally the phantom's feet would leave the ground and he would float along for a few yards before coming down and running in a plausible manner. At these times, Mark noticed, the girl's face lost its usual placid expression. Her training had prepared her for no such antics as these.

Once inside the wood they stopped and watched the settlement for signs of pursuit, but evidently the barbarians wanted no more to do with these unusual people.

"I tried out your suggestion," remarked the phantom, allowing the punctured body to fall to the ground and speaking from a point in the air where the head had been.

The young lady, who had seated herself comfortably, looked around, wide-eyed, but said nothing.

"You mean you destroyed your brain?"

"Yes, completely. It was a bit of a gamble, but I had to know."

Mark was silent for a moment. It seemed this goofy ghost had an awful wad of courage to risk extinction just to prove something that didn't need proving at all.

"Suppose you take another body now," he suggested, "and tell us how you happened to be occupying that other one."

With an abruptness that astonished even Mark, who was becoming used to such things, the phantom appeared in a brand new body, this one moderately handsome.

"You didn't have to try to look like an Adonis," Mark complained.

"So that's the way it is?" said the Adonis sagely, with a glance at the girl.

"Not exactly," Mark said nervously. "But just the same you might play fair, you know."

"Well, maybe this will suit you better." And so saying the

handsome physique began to age before their eyes. It was an infirm and decrepit Adonis who grinned at them now.

"All right. And stay that way," said Mark. "And now suppose you explain yourself. And while I think of it, suppose you give us a name. I'm tired thinking of you as the Goofy Ghost."

"You don't for a moment imagine I like to be thought of that way? It's insulting, that's what it is," declared the apparition in a quavering voice. "Suppose you call me 'Omega.' You couldn't say my real name. Wrong kind of vocal apparatus. And incidentally you two should really be introduced. Allow me to present Nona Barr, who recently ran away from home rather than marry a certain gentleman. Nona, I think you will find Mark Nevin a pleasant fellow, even if he is about six thousand years older than you."

NONA ACKNOWLEDGED the introduction with a little curtsy, and then for some reason incomprehensible to Mark, blushed a deep crimson. He grinned, hoping to put her at ease, but could think of nothing to add to his, "How do you do?" Nona, to cover her confusion, turned in wonderment to Omega.

"How did you know my name and that I ran away from home?"

"Been watching you since you were born. I knew the Eugenics Council had made another mistake when your mother and dad were married. You were bound to have that spark of independence that they have been so diligent in exterminating. So I watched you with interest, saw the spark flare up half a dozen times, and finally break into flame when they tried to marry you to that nincompoop."

At this point Mark interrupted with: "She can't understand that you have watched her all her life without knowing what sort of person you are. And while you're telling her that suppose you explain how I was asleep for six thousand years. She thought I was lying when I told her."

Omega thoughtfully removed the remains of his former body, explaining that he had acquired that lump of human clay by the simple expedient of copying one of those whom Mark had killed during his capture. He had then joined the marching captors, telling them that he had not been killed, but knocked out. As for being placed as Mark's guard, that had been a matter for volunteers and he had been the only one to offer.

Omega seemed to be wound up, for after exhausting the subjects of his own and Mark's history, he went on to describe to Mark the civilization of which Nona had been a member.

It was a socialistic sort of affair with certain governmental powers vested in various councils, These councils had the final authority in matters falling within their jurisdiction. Thus it happened that when the Eugenics Council had decided that a mate for Nona must have certain characteristics—known as "gene determinants"—and found that there was but one man who filled the bill, there was no choice for her but to take that man or run away.

"The idea itself is a good one," Omega stated, "if they had been intelligent enough to work it out properly. The rapid progress of my own civilization was partly due to careful selection. Supermen could be created in the same manner. But this council invariably misses the important characteristics and instead fosters such points as stoicism—which is commendable, but not particularly important—and the ability to knuckle down to superiors—which makes for unified action, but stifles independent thought. Taken by and large they have used eugenics for selfish purposes rather than for scientific progress.

"And don't get any funny ideas, Mark. Your genes wouldn't suit the council, either. They wouldn't even admit you. You'll just have to find somewhere else to go."

MARK GLARED savagely at the ground, and wished Omega had a little self-restraint. If there was any courting to be done, he'd do it himself, without any suggestions from an antiquated. Which reminded him that he was six thousand years old himself.

"And now that we are acquainted with each other," Omega was saying, "what's next on the program?"

"I'm hungry," Nona declared, after the fashion of women from time immemorial.

"Just a minute, and I'll see what's in the kitchen," Omega said, groaning as he hobbled toward a nearby patriarch of the forest.

"Where is he going?" inquired Nona. "He's a dreadful old man."

"I'm not going to try to predict anything he might do. But a good guess would be that he is going to step out from behind that tree with an armful of groceries. He's full of surprises."

But an armful of groceries was much beneath Omega's abilities. In a few minutes he came shuffling forth, carrying a table, heavily laden with food. Wisps of steam curled up from under silver covers and fragrant odors rose into the air. Two chairs floated madly through the air behind him.

"Don't show any sign of surprise," whispered Mark. "He's vain enough now."

Nona hastily composed her face and calmly sat down in a chair that Mark captured for her.

"Thank you," she said sweetly.

Omega looked searchingly at her, then at Mark, who was trying to hide a grin. "So that's it!" he exclaimed. "Spoiling my fun. We'll see about that."

Mark lifted the covers, one by one, and disclosed a series of dishes designed to whet the most jaded of appetites. Although he, strangely, had not been the least bit hungry since his awakening, the sight and aroma of this food made him ravenous.

"Now if you people will excuse me for a few minutes," Omega said, his body gradually fading as he spoke, "there is a little matter I must attend to."

CHAPTER VI

THE DANGEROUS BRAINS

THAT SHOULD HAVE warned Mark, but when the vanishing act was completed he forgot about his benefactor, and fell to helping Nona. Except for being slightly aggressive, the girl's table manners were reassuringly correct. Mark's first mouthful—a forkful of tender roast beef—revealed to him what Omega had in mind when he had said, "We'll see about that." The beef tasted like stewed onions! And Mark hated stewed onions.

A glance at Nona told him that she had noticed nothing wrong. Obviously this was Omega's work. Mark determined to eat the stuff if it killed him. The next mouthful—mashed potatoes laden with gravy—tasted like sour milk.

A roar of laughter blasted forth from a point nearby. Nona, startled, dropped her fork and stifled a scream.

"Don't be alarmed," Mark advised. "It's only Omega and his depraved sense of humor. He's making my food taste like swill and I'm eating it to spite him."

He conveyed another forkful to his mouth, prepared for anything. He was fooled this time. The beef tasted like beef. "It's all right now," he announced. "I guess he's left."

"I hope so," she said. "This food is so good, and he makes me nervous. I can't eat when I'm upset."

"He's not a bad sort," Mark declared, thoughtfully, "except for his habit of being as confusing as he can manage. But I guess we'll have to get used to it. He seems to be interested in both of us."

"Yes, so I've noticed."

Mark speared a slice of pickled beet. "There was something I meant to ask you," he said, trying to remember, and carrying the beet halfway to his mouth. "Oh yes.... How do you account for the fact that after several thousands of years your language is no different from mine, and yet that of those oafs in the village is just so much Greek?"

"That's simple," Nona said through a mouthful of mashed potatoes. "You see, after the last great war, records of which are preserved in our museum, my ancestors gathered in the ruins of a great city. They managed to survive on stored foodstuffs until they were able to grow their own. Some semblance of the former civilization was retained, for among them were wise and intelligent leaders.

"A government was organized and later a system of education instituted. Textbooks were found in the ruins, and they naturally preserved the written language; and phonograph records and machines for playing them were also discovered. Copies of these are still used today. And it has been the continued use of these ancient records which has preserved the language, though I dare say there are hundreds of words, of a technical nature, which have dropped out through disuse, and possibly some which have been created to meet new conditions."

"VERY LOGICAL," commented Mark, placing the slice of pickled beet, which had been hovering in mid-air, in his mouth. There followed an explosion of considerable violence, which was perfectly natural, in view of the fact that the beet had all the delicate flavor and bouquet of slightly used gunpowder. "Damn," said Mark, feeling to see if he'd lost any teeth.

Nona jumped to her feet, and bent over him solicitously. This anxiety over his welfare was not entirely unwelcome. In fact he rather liked it, though he was too honorable—or too stupid— to prolong it needlessly.

"I'm all right," he gasped. "That was Omega again. The darned clown fed me a firecracker. Omega," he shouted, "behave yourself, won't you please?"

Nona looked angrily about, but Omega remained unpleasantly invisible.

"I don't think it's fair," she said, stamping one foot. "He gives you this meal and then spoils it for you. Wait till I get my hands on him."

"Leave him alone," begged Mark. "Don't be fooled by that lad. He might have the sense of humor of a twelve-year-old, but he has brain-power such as the Earth has never seen. This stuff you have see him perform is only child's play. His tricks are the manipulation of the basic stuff of the Universe—matter and energy.

"Those bodies of his represent energy wrested from radiations which pervade space, and transformed into matter in exact duplication of the tremendously complex structure of the human organizer. No, there was never a brain like his developed on the Earth."

A modest cough came from behind them. There was Omega, superannuated as they had last seen him, looking very serious.

"You are wrong there, my friend," he stated. "There are two minds right now on this earth, each of which is as well equipped as I. I'll admit they are not natural but that doesn't alter the fact that they are very powerful."

"How are they not natural?" inquired Mark.

"**THEY'RE ARTIFICIAL,** of course," replied Omega, scornfully. "I'll tell you about it. A little less than six thousand years past—you were asleep at the time—a certain Russian biologist became aware that his life expectancy was nothing to brag about, due to the fact that his country was gradually being destroyed in the course of the last war, and decided upon a bold experiment.

"He had discovered the very same fluid that I had earlier developed for the purpose of preserving my brain and those others who were the last of my race. And he had also discovered how to join the nerve-ends of two brains so that one—the more powerful one—could blanket out the ego of the other and have control of both brains. His bold experiment consisted of hooking together in this manner twelve brains!

"For his key-brain he chose the preserved one of a former

laboratory associate who had met with an accident. This man had been exceptionally clever and the Russian hoped that he would gain control of the others, who were ordinary men and women.

"The biologist had no trouble acquiring these brains, for he was working directly for the government and was given all the condemned prisoners he wished, with which to experiment. He had duped officials into thinking that he was developing a new germ culture for use as a weapon, and needed live humans to try it on. His real purpose, of course, was to make himself immortal, which he actually did!

"The associate easily gained control of the other brains and soon found himself possessed of powers of which he had never dreamed. He suddenly realized that he had now regained all the senses he had been deprived of since his crushed body had been destroyed and the brain preserved.

"The twelve-brain-power mind was able to communicate, by means of thought waves, with the biologist, who informed him of his aims. These consisted of removing his own brain and connecting it with fifteen others and preserving the whole batch in a suitable container. The biologist, being a very selfish man, wanted to have the more powerful mind. The associate had been a very loyal workman when he was alive and had a certain amount of gratitude in his present state. He therefore agreed to perform the operation, but with only eleven brains.

"He didn't fancy the biologist being any more powerful than he, even if he was grateful. He didn't know then that the extra ones would have been of no use. His knowledge was still very limited. He was like a man who has suddenly lost his memory, but still has all his other mental faculties.

"He knows nothing, but has the power to reason and to acquire knowledge quickly. As a matter of fact, five brains connected in this manner would have given a maximum thought capacity. Intelligence was not increased by adding more."

"Wait a minute," Mark interrupted. "I know the biologist

needed help to remove his own brain, but how could the associate do it without any hands?"

"My, my, my," Omega said sadly, peering nearsightedly at Mark. "I gave you credit for more imagination. I'll show you. Now if you will look over there you will see a fully equipped surgical laboratory."

Mark turned his head and stared. Sure enough, there it was, operating table, trephining apparatus and a number of gadgets unfamiliar to him. On the table lay the sheeted figure of a man. Then, without any volition of his own, he found himself bending over the figure and operating!

In a matter of minutes his flying fingers, had caused the strange instruments to remove the entire dome of the skull and expose the palpitating brain within. Abruptly the whole layout vanished and he was looking into the slightly dazed brown eyes of Nona, who did not yet realize that it was Omega, controlling Mark's body, who had performed the operation.

Mark nodded. "Of course. I should have guessed. I'm stupid."

"Not at all," returned Omega. "The biologist was no more intelligent than you. He didn't know at the time he presented his problems to the associate that the feat could be accomplished so easily. He expected advice as to how to build a mechanical device for the purpose. But the operation was a success and both batches of brains are alive today, each thinking as a powerful unit."

FOR A minute no one spoke. The story, Omega's feats, in fact everything which had happened since Mark's appearance on Nona's horizon, seemed like a fantastic dream or a fairy tale. Things really didn't happen that way. The last real thing which had happened to her had been the reception she had been given by the savage tribes-people. She remembered that with a shudder.

But more disconcerting than any of the other weird happenings was the man, Mark.

There were no men like him in her experience. He was like

the heroes in the ancient stories. She remembered, with a delighted shiver, the way he had grinned when Omega introduced them.

The men in the city didn't grin. There was nothing to grin about. Even in their leisure moments, the men she knew thought of nothing but of how to do their work more efficiently, in order to please the overseers. That, of course, was the fault of the eugenics system. Subservience was bred into her people. It was not their fault. But it didn't alter the fact that they were very dull company.

"Then I suppose," Mark commented with labored irony, "that when you have tired of watching the amusing, but far from intellectual, pursuits of lesser people, you indulge yourself in communion with these great brains?"

"Far from it," denied Omega. "Neither is a character I should dare to cultivate. When they were mere men, they were ambitious and ruthless. And they remain the same. Both are greedy for knowledge, which is commendable in itself, but they have no decency in acquiring it.

"Several times they destroyed capable leaders of different communities just to see how well the people could make out without them. Malicious curiosity, and nothing more. Later they amused themselves by pitting one community against another in conflict. Actually enjoying the resultant suffering.

"No, my friend, I don't desire any communion with such as they. On other planets, in other galaxies, there are minds whom I admire and with whom I sometimes communicate. But these two earthborn monsters don't even know I exist. Lately they have left the people of this planet to their own devices, to acquire knowledge of other worlds. And everywhere they go their infernal experiments wreak havoc."

"But haven't you done anything about it?" inquired Mark. "Surely with your vast power, you could destroy them. They certainly deserve it."

Omega shook his head sadly. "I'll grant you they are still too young to cope with me individually, but combined I'm afraid they would be too much for me. I've never dared to take the chance. As it is, by keeping them in ignorance of my existence, I have frequently circumvented them when their insatiable appetite for creating trouble has threatened to ruin some promising civilization." Omega's mockery and irresponsibility had vanished; his tone had become that of a beset father, trying to protect his children.

"Well, something should be done," Mark insisted. "Suppose they come back and decide to give the Earth another going over? They do come back, don't they?"

"If you mean do they return periodically and inhabit their brains, as I used to do, the answer is yes, they do. It's a matter of psychology, I suppose. I know I should never have gotten the idea of destroying my brain if you hadn't suggested it. And naturally they have never thought of it either, and probably never will. So of course they will come back, just when, there is no way of knowing. Possibly not for centuries. It's nothing for you to worry about."

"No," Mark admitted, glancing at Nona. "I suppose not. It just occurred to me that as long as those two are in existence nobody could ever be sure of a quiet, decent life."

"What's the difference?" countered Omega, with a glance toward Nona. "You can't expect to live quietly and decently anyhow. Someone always pops up to gum the works." He beamed. "I remembered that phrase," he said proudly.

Mark didn't seem to hear him.

"Well, be that as it may," he said, "the idea enters my mind that it will be dark soon and we are totally unprepared to spend the night in these woods. We'd better rig up some sort of shelter. Unless of course, you'd like to transform yourself into a six-room bungalow."

Omega cocked a weather eye toward the sky which was already becoming slightly gray with approaching twilight. "It won't rain," he stated. "And it won't be cold. You don't need a shelter. I would advise that you travel in a general southerly direction. There is still an hour or more of light and the further away from our late friends the better."

"You speak as if you were leaving us."

"Don't feel too sad. I'll be back again when you least expect me."

Mark laughed. "I'll just bet you will."

"So long, Mark." The sly smile on the withered face died out and the eyelids dropped. Mark hesitated for a moment, then placed one finger on the bony chest and gave a light push. The stooped figure teetered and then fell with a thud. Nona stepped forward, alarmed, but he reassured her.

"He's just absent-minded. Forgot his body."

CHAPTER VII

NOCTURNE FOR TOMORROW

THE GOING WAS a bit rough in the new direction, but that fact didn't bother Mark in the least. Helping Nona over obstructions was just as pleasant a way of putting in his time as he could wish for. Her grateful smiles of thanks were ample payment for the scratches he got separating thorny undergrowth for her.

"Have you any idea at all where we are going?" he inquired.

Nona hesitated before answering. "I'm not sure, but I think the nearest place in this direction is New Haven. It is not directly south, but more to the west. We must not go there, though."

"Why not?"

"Because the city is friendly with mine and would keep me prisoner until they could return me to the council."

"We don't want that," Mark declared. "You said this city was New Haven. Then we should be somewhere south of Hartford.

Was that the city in which your ancestors settled?" He remembered New Haven on crisp fall afternoons. Feathered hats. Chrysanthemums. Programs for a quarter.

"Yes," she replied. "New Haven is our closest neighbor and we often send caravans to exchange goods. But I've never been there. Women are not allowed to travel. Only armed men make up the caravans."

The sky was growing darker and the little light which penetrated through the trees was scarcely sufficient to enable them to pick their way through the dense forest. Mark spotted a clear space, devoid of vegetation, beneath a giant evergreen. This, he decided, would make an ideal place to spend the night.

"It just occurred to me that it has been quite a time since I've done any tramping through a New England woods. So far today I've seen no dangerous wild life, except for those unpleasant cannibals. But of course that doesn't prove anything. How about it?"

Nona's eyes widened, he frowned. "Oh gracious, I thought you knew! There are wildcats—thousands of them! Nobody ever goes near the forest after nightfall. Even the armed caravans will travel miles out of their way to get away from them. But *you* can kill them, can't you? You're so wonderful. They won't come near us when you use your magic, will they?"

"Magic?"

"Yes, the magic that you used against the savages. You pointed your finger and they fell dead. Even Omega wasn't that smart. *He* had to use a club."

Mark winced realizing that the girl thought him some kind of wizard with all sorts of weird powers. He was flattered, of course, but sporadic caution caused him to try to get things on a reasonable plane. "That wasn't magic. All it was was this needle gun. It's so small you thought it was my finger. It shoots needles, tipped with poison that stuns the victim for several hours. Simple, see?

"But I'm afraid it might not work against wildcats. Maybe

the needles couldn't penetrate their fur. Maybe I'd better build a fire."

AS HE talked, he had been fumbling in his pockets, although he knew that he would find no matches. That was one thing the old doctor had not thought of. Or maybe he had. There might have been a means of making fire in one of the cabinets, an old-fashioned tinder box or some such contrivance, for ordinary matches would have crumbled to dust with the years. He hadn't searched as carefully as he might have. His fingers encountered a spare clip to fit the automatic he had lost. A sudden train of thought snapped him into action. Tinder box—gunpowder....

An eerie scream rose in the still air, sending a shiver down his backbone, and confirming Nona's story. Removing a cartridge from the clip, he used the point of a clasp-knife to pry the bullet loose. Then he carefully selected some dried leaves, crumpled them, and mixed in the powder from the brass cartridge. Some small, dried twigs completed the tinder. Then in the fast fading light he managed to find a hard rock, about the size of his hand.

"Hold your breath," he requested, and struck the blunt end of the steel axe a sharp blow. Nothing happened. "I should have joined the Boy Scouts," he mourned, striking another futile blow. The third, however, produced a shower of sparks, although none of them landed on the tinder. On about the tenth try the tinder flared with a sudden greenish flame and continued burning merrily while Mark piled on heavier twigs until he had a sizable blaze. He was surprised, naturally, but took care not to show it.

"That should do the trick," he said, satisfied. "We'd better fix up a place to sleep before it gets too dark. We can make a couple of soft mattresses if we collect enough of these leaves."

"I'll do that," Nona answered. "You hack off some branches with the axe and I'll strip off the leaves. Then we can use the wood for the fire."

Those Vikings, crowded around them, made
way for the oldster with the knife.

"Clever girl. Except that the wood, being green, would make more smoke than flame."

"I'm still clever," she retorted. "The smoke will discourage the mosquitoes. And there is enough dry wood within reach to keep the fire blazing."

"Oh-oh. Mosquitoes! I'd forgotten them. It's six thousand years since I've been bitten by one of the pesky critters."

With both of them working energetically it took very little time to collect enough dry wood, leaves and green wood. Fortunately there was but the lightest of breezes and the leaves were in no danger of blowing away. Nona busied herself with arranging them to form a thick matting while Mark chopped the wood into convenient lengths.

Finishing his task he surveyed the result of Nona's efforts with a quizzical eye. She had undoubtedly fashioned a comfortable bed. Not two beds—one bed. The leaves were spread out over a wide area, to a depth of about four inches.

Mark saw immediately that certain implications were staring him right in the eye, but for the life of him he couldn't come to any definite conclusion regarding them. Of course he realized that customs were bound to be changed.

But Nona had seemed to be such a nice girl.... He was just about to blurt out a leading question when he saw that she was standing beside her handiwork, smiling brightly, evidently expecting some sort of praise.

"Nice job," he said lamely, and turned to sit down near the fire. Look here, he addressed himself sternly, if I'm just going to sit around burdened with a flock of Twentieth Century ethics—but it was no good. He was, heaven help him, unsuspectedly puritanical.

Nona stood looking at Mark's back for a long minute before making up her mind what to do. Then she went over and sat beside him, following his gaze into the fire. The dancing flames seemed to conjure up a picture of a rugged young face just breaking into a smile. Startled, she stole a glance at its living counterpart, wondering if this were more magic or if her own thoughts of him caused her to see the image. But Mark was still staring gloomily into the fire.

"Dearest Mark," she whispered and ran her fingers through his hair. Mark jerked away. Had the creature no shame?

She hesitantly placed her hand on his arm. "Did I.... Is there anything wrong?" she asked timidly.

Mark smiled. He put a finger under her chin, tilted her head back, and looked searchingly into her eyes. "No," he declared. "Nothing. Not after the way you said that."

Nona smiled. "I'm glad. When you were sad, I was sad," she said, naively. "But something was wrong. Will you tell me?"

MARK TURNED again to stare at the fire before venturing to speak. There it was again. If one were to accept the girl's actions and words at their face value and judge them according to standards dead these thousands of years, one might reach a wrong conclusion. Mark's sense of values needed a hasty reconditioning—but he couldn't seem to get on with it.

With all the things that had happened since he had met her

it seemed that he had known her for years. And then there were times that he didn't know her at all.

"I'll tell you some other time," he promised, tossing a dry stick in the fire. He licked his lips and sought a reasonably safe topic of conversation. "Now suppose you tell me something of how people live in your city."

Nona shuddered. "They don't. They just exist. I don't mean there is any hardship," she explained. "It's just that life in the city is so monotonous. The people have no initiative. Even their pleasures are directed. And although the hours of work are not long, it always seems that there is no time to do things you want to do. There is always some meeting that you must attend, where stuffy people discuss ways to co-operate more efficiently so that more work may be accomplished in a shorter time. The reason given for this endless quest for efficiency, is to get more time for leisure. But there's not much sense to that if the people are allowed no leisure anyway.

"The Recreation Council insists that you relax according to directions. There are games, contests and all sorts of ways you may spend your own time. But you must decide just what you wish to do on any certain day, and then sign up for it. You can't change your mind at the last minute and do something else. You must appear at the designated recreation place and answer to your name and number. Otherwise you will be punished with extra work hours. I was punished often.

"There was only one recreation that I liked. We were given permission to read the reproductions of any of the ancient books we liked, and that is how I spent most of my time. You would think that when people read of the freedom enjoyed by their ancestors they would have been discontented with their lot. That was the effect it had on me. But just the opposite was true of the rest. They seldom read of the ancients, because it made them mad that their ancestors could have been so frivolous and selfish; so concerned with their individual welfare. So you see my people are really satisfied with the way they live. I was the only one who rebelled at having my every move plotted out for me."

"The little rebel, eh? And you didn't care for the husband they picked for you either."

THE EERIE wail of a nearby wildcat mingled with Nona's chuckle. "You should have seen him. They picked him because they thought he was stolid enough to counteract the wayward streak in me. There was no other man in the city so submissive and willing to obey. He was never so proud as when he was permitted to take part in some volunteer extra work. I remember the day the man from the Eugenics Council brought him to my father's house. We were introduced and I was told that this was the man the council had chosen for my mate. Then we were left alone. You see, it is the regular procedure when the council chooses two people to be mated to introduce them and then leave them alone for two hours to get acquainted. They then separate and the mating date is set for a day one week later.

"During this week either of the two may decide not to take the other for a mate. Then he or she is introduced to another who has the required gene-determinants. Each person is allowed five choices although seldom does anyone ask for a second choice. It's foolish to do so, for if one person has the same gene-determinants as another, he would differ from the other in only the most superficial characteristics. So there really isn't any choice at all."

"I suppose that after generations of such artificial selection your people would be pretty nearly alike anyway," Mark guessed.

"Oh yes," Nona said. "The art of photography has been almost abandoned. A picture of one man would do for all the men in the city." She chuckled again, and spread her hands. "That's an exaggeration, of course, for there are differences physically, but not nearly so much as I've noted in the pictures in the ancient books. No two people looked alike in those days, did they?"

"Very few," Mark admitted. "But what sort of a ceremony is held when two people are mated?"

"Ceremony?" Nona looked puzzled for a moment. "Oh, I know what you mean. I've read about it. We don't have anything like that. On the appointed day the couple are assigned a house and they occupy it. That is all."

Mark felt this was too direct to be any fun. He forgot, momentarily, that one reason he'd shunned marriage was his dread of a big church wedding.

"Like heck it is, but that's just what I suspected. Tell me some more." He threw another branch on the fire at the sound of a raucous screech. "Do these couples live happily together?"

"Happily? Oh yes, I suppose so. It seemed rather dreary to me. You see, they don't live together in the sense that the ancients did. Neither sees the other except when the day's work and recreation is over. And that amounts to only about ten hours, which includes the sleeping period."

Mark thought this one over a minute. "Pretty clever," he decided. "They don't see enough of each other to quarrel. Not a bad stunt at that. The men are segregated from the women at all other times, I suppose?"

"Yes, of course, Since I was a little girl the only men I have spoken to have been my father, the man from the Eugenics Council and the rabbitlike little slug I was introduced to. I only saw the last two for a few minutes."

Mark grinned. "And Omega and me," he supplemented. "Although Omega is not a man. He's a perambulating thought wave. And what happened to your would-be mate?" Not that he cared—or did he?

NONA ROCKED back and forth, her hands clasped about her knees. "He looked at me, displayed about thirty-one teeth, and said nothing; I think he was scared. I scowled at him and said, 'Scram, you worm.' But I don't think he understood, for he just stood there, the grin fading into a sickly-looking smirk. But he got the idea quickly enough when I opened the door and kicked him out. Quite hard. He went out so fast that be almost stepped on the heels of the Eugenics man. You see I don't know many men. I sometimes wish I did. I think I'd like men a lot. Women are so dreadfully stupid. But maybe you don't think so." She smiled a carbolic smile, and watched his face anxiously.

Mark gazed thoughtfully into the flames. His gloom almost returned, but he shook it off. "No, I can't say I do," he admitted, noncommittally.

Nona smiled irritably. "I didn't think so. But things were different then. People were free! But those others don't matter now. Or...." A sudden thought seemed to paralyze her. It was a minute before she spoke. "Tell me. Was there anyone.... Did you have a mate?" The last words came all in a breathless rush.

Mark looked sharply at her, and then grinned. "No," he assured. "Almost, but not quite."

Nona was silent for a long time. Then suddenly she said: "Did you love her? I know about love. The old books explained it, but I really never understood until...." She stopped abruptly, evidently influenced again by something she had read.

Mark hesitated. "I'm not so sure I know the answer to that one. I thought I loved her, and I certainly was miserable when she married someone else at the last minute. But I'm not miserable any more, so it's just possible that my emotion wasn't really love. Funny, though. It was hell for a while.... Don't ask me. I was never an expert at love, I guess. It only happened once and I'm not so sure just what did happen."

The combined wails of two or three wildcats rent the evening stillness from a point not far away. Mark looked around at the deep shadows that ringed the little clearing, but saw no sign of the cats. Later, perhaps, there would be the glowing reflections from their eyes, but he was sure that none would venture within the lighted area.

"Maybe you'd better go to sleep now," he suggested. "I'll keep the fire going."

"I'm not sleepy. I'd rather talk." She drew closer to Mark and, at the dictates of an uncomfortably acute conscience, he retreated.

"It seems to be a peculiarity of your sex," he commented. "But I still think you should sleep. You've had a hard day and tomorrow might be harder." Tonight, the Lord knew, apparently was going to be trying enough. His arms ached now with the will to hold them at his side.

"But so have you," she insisted. "You sleep and I'll watch. I read somewhere that it is the woman's duty to serve the man." Her smile was utterly childlike and completely irresistible.

"Huh," Mark said, very weakly. "Don't believe all you read, young lady. There have been some crackpot philosophers with peculiar ideas concerning human relations. One—possibly the one you read—believed that women should serve men like slaves. He spoke of his ideal man as a 'superior' man, who, it seems, was one who demanded much but gave little. Things don't work out that way, fortunately. His 'superior' man would have to be a cold, supercilious sort of a critter, and people just don't take to that kind of person, even women, who are known to be peculiar at times. Instead of serving, a woman would be more apt to hate him. People don't do things because they should do them; they do things because they *want* to. As soon as an act is considered a duty, people want to do the opposite." It didn't make much sense, Mark thought wildly, but when you talk you can't kiss....

Nona thought it over for a minute. "Yes, I understand. But you see, I want to watch the fire for you."

Mark looked disgusted, and felt entirely helpless. Nona looked into his eyes with an expression that told him exactly where he stood, then seeing that he was scowling she appeared very contrite.

"Is that wrong?" she asked. "There is so much I must learn. Please tell me and don't be angry."

Mark promised to wake her when he got sleepy and let her take a turn at playing watchman. In spite of her scanty attire she insisted that she would not get cold, but Mark made her take his jacket for covering. The fire would keep him warm, although the night seemed to be mild enough to warrant no protection from the elements. He replenished the blaze and looked about for some visible evidence of the cats, whose wailing was making a constant cacophony in the almost motionless air. This time he saw a pair of glowing points, apparently suspended in mid-air, above the thick branch of a nearby tree. He snatched a burning brand from the fire and tossed it at the eyes. They disappeared amid a shower of sparks, to the accompaniment of a hideous spitting and hissing.

"And that takes care of you, my fuzzy friend," he remarked, retrieving the brand and tossing it back into the fire.

CHAPTER VIII

BLUEBLOOD

LATER, WHILE OCCUPYING himself by hacking absently at a piece of wood with his clasp-knife, Mark was jolted by a startling discovery. An unexpected slip of the knife caused it to slice a thin sliver of flesh from his knuckle. The blade was so keen that he didn't immediately notice the slight wound, and continued whittling until startled by the sight of blood. Mark was not one to be awed, dismayed or even annoyed at the loss of a few drops of blood. But this time he was definitely alarmed when he noted the injury. For the blood was not red. It was blue!

Wiping a few drops from the cut with a finger he moved closer to the fire to be sure his eyes were not playing him false. The blood was blue, as deep blue as it had been red! There could be no doubt; no trick of reflected light was causing this phenomenon. Hastily he examined the wound from which it had oozed. He couldn't find it.

In that short time the wound had healed, and new skin

covered the place where the old had been sliced off! He found the place, finally, but except for the fact that the new skin was a shade whiter than that surrounding it, there was no sign of the cut. Mark hadn't minded Omega's tricks; as a spectator he had even been olympically amused. But if his body was going to go gay on him—Mark suddenly thought of the scratches he had suffered on the backs of both hands while helping Nona through the brambles. There was no sign of these either. He remembered thinking at the time that the pain incurred was of surprisingly short duration, whereas the scratches should have smarted for quite a while. He hadn't looked then because he hadn't wanted Nona to notice.

This discovery and the fact that for the first time he had time to think, started a train of thought that was to leave him even more puzzled. He remembered that after the initial surprise at his surroundings, his first physical sensation had been thirst. Not hunger; just thirst.

There had been no feeling of cold in spite of the fact that he had been nude. He had only donned clothes for reasons of modesty and to have a place to carry weapons. Further he remembered that when he washed in the water from the jug there had been no shock from the cold contact although he had doused himself thoroughly. He had felt the change in temperature, but not nearly so acutely as he used to before the long sleep.

Of course he had been so filled with wonder at the antics of Omega at the time, that he might not have been so sensible to sensation as normal. As an experiment he rolled up a sleeve and placed the end of a glowering brand within a few inches of his arm. There was plenty of heat, and the hair curled up, singed, but he felt no pain!

Gritting his teeth he placed it in direct contact with the skin, then drew it quickly away. A grunt escaped his lips when the flesh seared for an agonizing instant.

But the pain left almost as quickly as it came, and the burned spot healed over without forming a blister. He brushed the charred portion and the dried skin flaked off to reveal an arm unmarked, save for the little charred circle of singed hair.

For a moment or two he just stared at his arm.

His thoughts went back over the events of the day.

He remembered the spear-prods given him by the cannibals marching him to their village. But the effected portion was so situated that he decided—with a glance toward Nona, who might wake up at any minute—to forego the inspection of that part.

Then, of course, there was hunger. He hadn't experienced any at all, though he had always been a heavy eater. He had eaten, all right, but only after the odors of Omega's dinner had made his mouth water. And that was more from habit than need, for he had only eaten a few mouthfuls.

Contemplation of it all made his head swim. The changed blood, with its bluish color, was no doubt the result of the anaesthetic given him before the operation. The anaesthetic had been injected, he recalled.

Of course, it might just be that his aristocratic ancestry was manifesting itself, he mused, with a grin at the dancing flames. He'd have to ask Omega about it. The peculiar blood was probably the cause of the other physical changes he had noted; the quick healing, the dulling of pain, the lessened—or perhaps nonexistent—need for food, and....

Jumpin' Jehosaphat! He suddenly realized that he should be dead tired by now. But he wasn't. He had no desire to sleep, at all. In spite of miles of walking, a fight, and enough excitement to last him a year, be felt no vestige of weariness....

HE HAD just begun to feel elated at his new powers when this thought struck him. But he didn't feel so chipper when he contemplated the long nights ahead of him, during which he very much feared he would get fed up with his own company. On the other hand he had eaten, when he evidently didn't require food, so possibly he could sleep if he so desired. He almost awakened Nona in his anxiety to try out this theory, but the sight of her made him decide not to.

He bent over her and replaced the jacket which had shifted and partly uncovered her beautifully formed body. A leaping flame revealed a smile that gave her features a radiance that could only be surpassed, Mark was thinking, by the splendor of her luminous eyes.

Perversely he recalled thinking the same thing of another beautiful lady. But that one had been grossly sophisticated, shamefully mercenary. He had found that out almost too late; but he knew now that Nona was touchingly and oddly naive.

Resuming his vigil at the fire, Mark's thoughts returned to the puzzle of his changed condition.

There must be some other answer to this queer lack of hunger. Maybe it was merely temporary loss of appetite, though one would think that he would lack energy if that were the case.

Any machine, human or otherwise, must be supplied with fuel or it ceases to function. Output can't be greater than input. And the energy he had put forth during the day far surpassed the amount of food energy he had consumed. But then, there were machines, equipped to store energy in advance for future consumption. The human machine had that ability.

But that couldn't apply to this instance. For two days prior to the appendix business he hadn't been able to eat because of the pains in his abdomen. That would be enough to weaken a man without having to undergo an operation.

And yet he had gone under the knife, lived without further nourishment for six thousand years, and then gone out and put in a strenuous day. And still felt no fatigue. Curiouser and curiouser.

He hoped Omega would know the answer.

CHAPTER IX

WHEN IS A BEAR....

WITH THE MORNING'S slow advance the weird wailings gradually lessened until they finally ceased. This particular breed of cats appeared to be entirely nocturnal in habit. A curious rabbit hopped into the clearing and inspected the girl's sleeping figure, ignoring Mark. This was an error on the bunny's part, for Mark declined to ignore him. A well-aimed stone put an end to the rodent's curiosity. Nona stirred and jumped to her feet as she realized that Mark had allowed her to sleep the night through.

"You broke your promise," she said, looking as pretty as two pictures.

"No, I didn't," he grinned. "I promised to wake you when I got sleepy. And I didn't get sleepy."

"But you must have. I was exhausted."

"But you forget I am a very unusual person," he reminded her. "Suppose you just rest over here while I get breakfast."

"But that isn't right," she protested. "I read that the custom in your day was for the woman to prepare the food for the men."

Mark sighed. "Yes, but do you know how to skin a rabbit and cook it over an open fire?"

"No," she admitted, ashamed.

"Well I do. So you just sit there and marvel. By the way, who does do the cooking in your city?"

"It's not my city!" she flared, then calmed down instantly. "The cooking is done by groups of men whose only duty is to prepare meals for the other workers. The city is divided into sectors, and in the center of each sector is a community building. At meal times long tables are set up.

"Men eat first, leave the building, and fifteen minutes later the women eat. The children are fed in a separate hall in the samc building. Thece children's halls are attended by groups of women, although the food is prepared by the regular cooks. This community form of eating was adopted because of economy and also because it insured equality. It saves time, too."

"Also very clever on the part of the city fathers. The family dinner table offers too much opportunity for private discussion of affairs of state. And the men do all the cooking, eh?"

"Oh yes. I have heard that the women once did that work, but it was found that men could work together more efficiently and with less disagreement."

Mark chuckled. "Restaurant and hotel owners knew that thousands of years ago."

Nona was absorbedly watching the process of preparing the rabbit. Occasionally she would ask a question, but for the most part she was silent, missing not a movement of Mark's capable hands. And she could not have had a better tutor when it came to cooking game, for he had spent a good portion of his former existence on hunting and camping trips.

The rabbit was finally done to a turn and Mark dismembered it.

"Next time I'll be able to cook the meal," Nona said, between mouthfuls.

AN HOUR later found them resuming their journey southward. Neither had the slightest idea where they were going, for no plans for the future had been mentioned. Mark had given the matter some thought, but held his own council until he could get certain things straightened out in his mind.

For the present, he was aware, there was nothing he would rather be doing than strolling along with his delightful companion. And as long as she seemed to agree, the future was a nebulous thing, stretching out endlessly before them, not requiring any immediate thought.

But Mark's thoughts were not concerned with the future. He was still worried about Nona's calmly wanton behavior of the night before. There was the business of the bed of leaves;

the fact that her people made no ceremony of marriage; the way she referred to the duties of a woman toward a man, as gleaned from the old books; and finally her general attitude that every thing was quite settled between them and to be taken for granted.

That was what puzzled him most, for he didn't remember having said anything that might have been construed as leading toward matrimony, although, he privately admitted, the thought had never been far from his mind since their first meeting.

But the very fact that she seemed to have the situation all cut and dried in her mind made him wary. And then, too, he might be assuming too much. You could get into trouble that way, he remembered.

"I would offer a penny for your thoughts if I knew what a penny was," Nona remarked.

"I wouldn't swindle you. But you can tell me something, just what were you thinking, immediately after Omega introduced us?"

Ecstasy illumined her face. "I was so bewildered that at first I couldn't understand. You see my studies had given me the impression that in your time it was customary for the man to—I can't think of the right words. Oh yes—to 'pay court' to the woman of his choice.

"I'm not sure just what that means, but it doesn't matter. That was probably from a book written before your era. So I didn't realize for a moment, that Omega was really introducing us. Of course, he told me afterward that he had watched over me since I was born, and that he knew more than the Eugenic Council. But I didn't know that when he introduced us. All I could think of was that you wanted me. Your grin told me that. I was so happy I couldn't think."

Mark leaned over, cupped her chin in his hand, and kissed her. Lingeringly. "A little formality I overlooked," he explained.

The whole thing was now clear. To Nona an introduction

amounted to a giving in marriage. Here all the time he had been married to her—and without knowing it!

And what was even more astounding, she seemed to have been exceedingly happy about the situation from the first. All the while he had been afraid that he might be misinterpreting her actions. He suddenly frowned. The disturbing thought had to do with the conventional processes observed during his earlier days on the earth. Marriage was a matter to be performed by means of certain rituals.

Of course, this introduction affair was strictly regular in this day and age and evidently Nona considered it to be all that was required.

He stopped to analyze the process. In his day marriage was performed when a couple announced to the world, by answering questions put to them by a third person, that each took the other for a mate.

And in effect, this newer system amounted to practically the same thing. The witness is the person who does the introducing. And if the couple are satisfied with each other they announce it to the witness, and the world in general, by not demanding a substitute spouse. All very simple.

Well if Nona was satisfied, he was.

And now, it appeared, there were definite things which must be done. He was no longer a shiftless bachelor, but a settled married man. He would have to act like one and find a place to settle.

This general southerly direction that Omega had suggested should land them on the seacoast at a point several miles northeast of present-day New Haven. According to Nona there were no other seacoast settlements in this direction. Acting on this information he changed their course a bit to the eastward, in order that they reach the coast somewhere opposite the tip of Long Island. That should be a safe place to establish a home. All humans were apt to be enemies and therefore it was best to stay well clear of cities.

THEY HAD covered several miles ignoring the passage of time when Mark noticed that the sun seemed to be near the zenith. Although he had eaten very little of the roasted rabbit, the pangs of hunger didn't appear. This phenomenon had ceased to intrigue him and in fact he had decided to eschew eating altogether, unless he should get hungry.

There was no use in going to the bother, as long as this new blood of his continued to rejuvenate itself. He realized that as time went on he would even cease to be stimulated by the sight or odors of food. And that was really no loss, for although in the past he had certainly enjoyed eating satisfying meals, it was obvious that if he hadn't needed the food he wouldn't have found any pleasure in eating it.

After the first few bites of the meal that Omega had furnished—those bites which hadn't tasted like garbage—the artificially stimulated appetite had left him. But for all that, he suddenly thought, Nona required food and it was up to him to procure some.

This might turn out to be quite an undertaking, he realized, for aside from the needle-gun he had only his axe for a weapon. Rabbits were plentiful, but a lucky throw like that one this morning couldn't always be duplicated.

They had sighted deer twice and an axe could be used to kill a deer, but the trouble was to induce the animal to come close and hold still while you performed the operation.

A bow and some arrows seemed to be indicated, except that even if he could construct a workable bow, it would take too long, and then he wouldn't know how to use it.

Thus gloomily meditating, Mark was startled by a thrashing in the nearby underbrush. The sound appeared to be coming toward them. Motioning Nona to be quiet he grasped the handle of his axe and crouched, ready to spring into action. This, he fervently hoped, would be a deer, and there would be darned little time in which to do the slaughter.

Sweat made the handle of the axe slippery but he was afraid

to relinquish his grip for the instant needed to wipe it. The deer might appear during that instant. The threshing sound came nearer.

Abruptly the underbrush parted and out waddled the largest brown bear he had ever seen. Bear steaks were good to eat.

Mark moved lithely forward, axe poised for one killing blow. There might not be time for a second. Bears were not apt to cherish a person with bear steaks on his mind. But this particular specimen didn't seem to be unduly alarmed. He merely raised up on his hind legs and stood waiting while Mark advanced.

With a sudden shift to the left to dodge the outstretched paws, Mark swung a terrific blow. But the sharp movement of the axe caused the slippery handle to turn in his hand.

The intended shearing stroke which should have come close to decapitating the great beast, became a harmless thump with the broad side of the blade.

The bear grunted in surprise and fell down on all fours, his unexpected movement wrenching the axe out of Mark's grasp. The weapon fell to the ground while his rush carried Mark several feet past the bear. The monster seemed unaware that he could easily polish off this bold antagonist, for he ignored Mark for the moment to satisfy his curiosity concerning the axe.

AFTER A few sniffs he picked it up with his teeth and carried it to Mark. Dreamily, Mark accepted the axe, at which the bear reared up and stood still as if offering to continue the game. Mark looked helplessly at Nona, and stuffed the axe back in his belt.

"I'll have to find you something else to eat," he told her, eyeing the bear, who looked about as ferocious as his smaller cousin, the teddy. "You can't kill anything that wants to play, the way this fool brute does."

Nona, who had been watching with one hand muffling her mouth, gave a great sigh and sat weakly on the ground. Bears were an item completely outside her experience, and the encounter had unnerved her somewhat. Mark helped her to her feet and they resumed their trek. The bear, in a friendly manner, trotted along at their heels.

"I hope it doesn't occur to that critter just what I was trying to do," Mark said, looking nervously over his shoulder.

Nona's eyes widened, "Is he dangerous?"

"I don't think so, judging by the way he acted when I tried to kill him. But on the other hand, he could be. I wish I wasn't so tender-hearted. I couldn't have missed a second time. But he looked so darned agreeable.... He thought it was all a game."

Nona was looking adoringly up at Mark's face, though doing so made her stumble, when both of them became aware that the breeze was carrying with it the tantalizing odor of fresh-cooked food.

Mark made a motion for quiet, and they advanced cautiously. No telling who might be responsible for the smell, but he had never heard of wild animals cooking their food, so it looked as if there might be humans in the offing. And humans were almost certain to be hostile.

But he was wrong this time. In a little clearing there was a table heaped with silver-covered dishes. It was only set for one, although there were three chairs. Omega was not in evidence but Mark suspected that he was there just the same.

"Well, the food problem seems to be solved for the present," he remarked. "Now if that pet poodle of ours doesn't decide to occupy the third chair.

But as if his words put the idea into the bear's head, the shaggy beast bounded on ahead of them and made a clumsy attempt to sit down on one of the chairs. Not being designed to support such a weight, the chair promptly collapsed. But the bear, nothing daunted, squatted on his haunches, which brought him to the proper height anyway. Mark, at this point, began to suspect that all was not as it seemed.

"Pay no attention to the clown," he told Nona, holding her

chair. "And if he lays a paw on anything you want, slap him one."

"But aren't you going to eat? There is only one plate."

Mark didn't answer, glaring at the bear, who was now looking very sullen, as if his feelings were hurt.

"He doesn't have to eat," the bear said, sulkily, in a high tenor voice.

"You might at least be a bass," Mark reproved.

"Did you ever hear a bear speak in a bass voice?"

"No. Never heard one speak at all."

"Well then, any kind of a voice I use is all right. And I'm getting sick and tired of your everlasting criticism. You're just jealous—that's all. Well, how've you been?"

"Okay. But you might have let me know you were marrying us. I didn't find it out until this morning. I must say I think it pretty inconsiderate...."

CHAPTER X

I TOOK THIS WOMAN

A HEARTY GUFFAW shook the bear's sides. Nona, who had dropped her fork when the bear began to speak, sighed and resumed her meal. Things didn't happen according to any fixed pattern any more and she was beginning to find, a sort of naturalness in the unexpected. But she wished Omega would leave them alone. There seemed to be some connection between him and the unusual things she had noticed about her husband. His not eating or sleeping, for instance. And besides, when the two of them got to talking, she couldn't understand a word.

"Well," Omega was explaining, "I could see that you would be weeks getting around to it by yourself, so I thought I would help out. And both your minds were already made up on the subject, except that you didn't know it. So I speeded things up for a very good reason. You have probably noticed that you are changed somewhat?"

"Yes. I meant to ask you about that."

"You have seen your blood?"

"Yes. It's blue. How come?"

"I'll explain. Keep your ears open, Nona. This concerns you, too. The cause of the change was the injection of the anaesthetic. The doctor concocted the thing mainly from a slightly radio-active compound which had been recently discovered. The resultant fluid resembled in some ways the liquid in which my brain was preserved, though differing in its effects. The anaesthetic action, of course, was only incidental. That really amounted to shock. The nervous system was numbed by the unaccustomed bombardment of radio-emanation, resulting in coma."

"But how is it that the guinea pig recovered consciousness, and I didn't? Was a different fluid used?"

"No. Same stuff. But the animal's greater vitality and coarser nerve sensitivity caused him to awaken after a few hours. You never would have woke up if I hadn't decided to help you. You would have lain there, half alive, for a few more thousand years, and then you would have died when the strength of the radio-active emanations decreased below a certain point. As it is you may live those years in full possession of your faculties."

Mark was stunned. This was something he was not prepared for. The implications involved evidently struck Nona a blow, for she let out a despairing wail.

"Then Mark will go on being a young man, while I grow old and ugly and...."

Omega raised a paw to silence her. "Nothing of the kind. That is what I was coming to. I think I told you that I have never made a practice of interfering with the life forms that I have found in my travels. Only on rare occasions I have helped promising civilizations when some catastrophe threatened them. But in this case I am making an exception. I have decided to create a new race of humans! And you two are to begin it.

"I expended a lot of thought before going ahead with it. The human race is a scurvy gang, as you probably know, with faults that far outnumber its virtues.

"Now don't look at me that way, Mark. If you will judge humans from an unbiased viewpoint, you must admit that they have hardly earned even the right to existence. Not speaking of individuals, mind you. There have been some noble and unselfish humans. But as a race they certainly deserve to be exterminated.

"They have repeatedly stamped out other life forms for no good reason; they have countless times reached high states of civilization, only to degenerate back to the beast. And all through human history travels the specter of cruelty, barbarism and senseless violence."

Mark was a bit miffed. "You're a little hard on us, aren't you? There is much to be said on the other side of the question."

"Not as a race, there isn't. But as individuals, something might be said for some of you. The only trouble is that your decent attributes usually become submerged. However, I suppose there's enough good in you to go on with. You two are to start a new life together, possessed of transmissible physical characteristics that should found a race capable of higher attainments than ever possible to ordinary humans. Oh yes, I am going to inject Nona to make her as you are. I'll do that now."

THE BEAR abruptly vanished and in its place was the patriarch they'd seen before. In his hand was a large hypodermic syringe.

"Whoa, Tillie," cried Mark. "I don't want her to go to sleep for six thousand years!"

"She won't. I'll strengthen her system to stand the shock."

The needle was inserted and its fluid pumped into the blood stream. Nona gave no sign that she felt anything. And, knowing Omega's powers, it is doubtful if she did.

"Now she has, or will have in a few hours, all the life vitality that has been yours since your awakening."

"What is the principal behind this change in blood?" inquired Mark.

"Scientists back in your time were beginning to suspect that life was dependent on radioactivity. They spoke of life-charges which they called radiogens. Fundamentally they were on the right track. There had to be something besides the ordinary working chemistry of the body to explain the behavior of metabolism.

"The process might be summed up by saying that at birth a creature of protoplasm is endowed with a certain quantity of life-charges. The radioactivity of these charges is so slight as to be almost nonexistent, but is nevertheless sufficient to support the life of the organism.

"As you know, radioactive materials are continuously breaking down into other elements. As this occurs the emanations decrease. Applying this to the organism you can see that as the radioactivity lessens, the vitality also lessens, metabolism slows down and the organism finally dies.

"In the case of your new blood, the radioactive element is much stronger and has a much longer half-period. The injection of the compound has changed your body chemistry considerably and given you certain physical properties which should ensure the survival of the new race.

"Food you will never need, because your blood always contains more energy than you can use in the everyday operation of your body. Ordinary injuries will scarcely pain, they will heal so quickly. And no disease germ can withstand the emanations of the compound.

"And while I think of it, you can heal germ diseases in others merely by bringing a portion of your body, your hands, for instance, into close proximity. The emanations extend a foot or so outside your body in sufficient strength to kill bacteria. You might be able to use that knowledge sometimes. Any questions?"

"Yes. I'm still wondering about the guinea pig. Why didn't the doctor notice these things in him?"

Omega chuckled. "He didn't get a chance. The animal only lived for a week after the injection. An overgrown tom-cat made a meal of him. The cat lived to a ripe old age, dying when about sixty, with the help of an Airedale."

Mark pondered for a minute. "You're sure these properties will be inherited?"

"Oh yes. It's not a matter of chromosomes, but life-charges, transmitted through the mother."

"Well then how does she get them to transmit? She has only a certain amount to start with."

"Look, son. I don't know everything. That's one of the things I'm not certain about. But I can tell you this: There is a race of beings, in another galaxy, who have your present form of life chemistry. They live for thousands of years and have similar reserves of vitality. And they transmit the quality to their off-spring. Therefore, you will.

"The difference, you must realize, is not one of body chemistry, although that is changed, but lies rather in the strength of the radioactive life-charges. Therefore if you can answer why ordinary humans can transmit their life-charges to their progeny, then you can answer the other question. I only know they do.

"A good theory is that your radiogens are being continually bolstered and augmented through absorption of the subcosmic energies which pervade space. That might explain why females of almost any species usually have greater vitality than males. Your insurance companies knew that women live longer than men and retain their vital powers later in life. Females must, therefore, be better equipped to absorb energy for the purpose of transmitting it to progeny.

"My knowledge of the thing might be compared with your knowledge of electricity. You know how to create it, use it and store it. You know all its properties, but you can't tell me what it is! As for me—I can create life, make it assume a number of forms, but for the life of me I can't tell you what enables the life-form to pass on the spark to its progeny. Absorption of energy is the only answer; but *how*, I don't know."

MARK DIGESTED this, thoughtfully, and decided that it sounded logical. But after all, logical or not, the fact that he and Nona had these wonderful powers was more important than the why and wherefore of how they worked. "Well, now that you have started the ball rolling, have you any further plans for us?"

"No. Just live your lives as you wish or as you may. But just remember that you are not limited to three score years and ten. You have plenty of time. I think half of the world's evil can be laid at the doors of people who were willing to sacrifice others that they might cram two lifetimes into the short one allotted them. Your progeny will grow up with the heritage of a long life, and that, coupled with the finer mental characteristics with which you will endow them, should form the nucleus for a great race. Well, good luck. I'm leaving for the time being. By the way, can you speak Swedish?"

"No. What's that got to do with it?"

With a twinkle in his eyes, Omega quietly faded in the manner of the Cheshire cat. "You'd be surprised," came his quavering voice, as from a distance.

"Disconcertin' cuss," Mark complained. "Do you feel any different?"

Nona, who by this time was becoming accustomed to Omega's abrupt comings and goings, was looking at him with a speculative gleam in her eyes. "No," she stated. "But that is unimportant. I gathered from a remark you made—that you were totally unaware what Omega meant when he introduced us. Is that right?"

Mark's jaw dropped. He hadn't credited her with such perspicacity. "Yes," he finally admitted, "I didn't know then."

"That's what I thought. But what I want to know is: Did you really want this to happen?"

"You mean for us to be married? Sure I did! But I didn't know how you felt. So I owe Omega a whole lot for settling the thing."

Nona's face brightened. "Then I was right about the 'paying court' that the old books told of."

"Oh yes. It was quite the thing in those days. One of the most popular all-around sports."

"And didn't the men tell the women how much they loved them?"

"Yes indeed. Although that came toward the end."

"Then you should tell me. Especially since we are already married."

"Of course, Nona." His voice grew solemn in spite of himself. "I love you with all my heart. I thought you knew that."

"I wanted to hear it. And maybe you had better kiss me. I don't want to have to do all the wooing."

CHAPTER XI

THE MAN FROM OSLO

IN THE YEAR 7966 forests covered most of the area which had once comprised the New England states. Thus it was that when Mark and Nona finally broke out of the woods' dark corridors they found themselves on a narrow strip of rocky beach facing the Atlantic Ocean.

For some time before the water was sighted they had heard the thundering of the breakers and felt the change in the air. But when the sea itself met their vision neither could speak for a moment.

After the disappearance of Omega, they had debated the question of the immediate future at some length. And now, in the late afternoon, the only decision they had come to was that they would establish a camp somewhere near the shore.

Later, Mark contended, it would be wise to seek a more southerly spot for the winter.

It was out of the question to return to the tomb for more supplies. Even granting he could find it, there was the ever-present possibility that they would be recaptured by the wandering savages. And that was too great a risk, now that he had Nona to consider. But the whole matter was shortly taken out of his hands, so he might as well not have worried.

A mile or so to the north was a rocky prominence jutting out almost to the water's edge. From that distance details could not be made out clearly, but it seemed to Mark that the lower fifteen feet of the cliff was in deep shadow. That might indicate that this lower portion was of soft rock which had been worn away some time in the past by the action of water, and now formed a recess sheltered by the overhanging cliff. It was well worth investigating, and they set out in its direction.

The forest receded as they approached the prominence, leaving a fairly wide beach. The cliff was indented deeply around the bottom. Mark didn't have time to notice any more because he saw something a lot more interesting. Emerging from the woods at a point skirting the cliff was a large body of decidedly odd-looking men. Mark gaped, rubbed his eyes until they stung and gaped again. But the men didn't disappear. And unless all the pictures in all the history books he'd ever seen were lying, the men were full-blown Vikings.

Big, rawboned, yellow-bearded bucks they were, with leather trappings, and most of them even bigger and heavier muscled than he. Their weapons seemed to consist of the short-sword and double-bitted battle-axe.

As yet the band had not sighted them and Mark bustled Nona toward the nearest fringe of forest. There would be a chance of eluding them once within the darkening wood, but they would surely be overwhelmed if they were caught out on the open beach.

Dusk was falling fast and it appeared for a moment as if they would not be discovered. The direction from which the Norsemen were approaching would make it impossible to escape if the band chose to intercept their flight. But still Mark was afraid to break into a run for the reason that a swiftly moving body is far more apt to be seen out of the corner of the eye than a slow-moving one. So they proceeded at a walk, in a direction at right-angles to the nearing band of men, each step bringing them closer to the safety of the forest.

BUT JUST about this time a particularly nasty Fate decided to insert a skinny finger and stir the brew. One of the nearer Norsemen glanced away from his course skirting the cliff and saw them. A sudden shout announced that they were discovered.

"Run for it!" he cried.

But he knew as he sped across the sifting sand, matching his pace with Nona's, that the Vikings had far less space to travel in order to cut them off. The race was lost before it was begun.

There was one last chance, however. "Nona! Cut across to the left. I'll engage them for a minute, and then catch up to you."

"No!—They'll kill you!"

"I can run faster than you," he explained. "I'll only need to stop them for a minute, and then I'll break away and catch up to you. Do as I say!"

Nona reluctantly obeyed. But the maneuver was spotted by the Norsemen, for two men detached themselves from the band and galloped off to catch the girl before she could reach the forest. Mark gave a groan and caught up to her. It was better to be together if this was to be the end.

And then too, if the Norsemen were in one body he could put more of them out of commission with the needle-gun, before the remainder could cut loose with their swords and axes. He only hoped that the gun would throw needles with sufficient strength to penetrate their leather trappings.

Instructing Nona to make a sudden bolt for the forest when the marauders drew near, Mark slowed his pace and loosened his axe in its holster. The needlegun he held in readiness.

In another second they would be in range. Aiming carefully at a level with their faces he released the trigger. The gun vibrated with a humming sound and one of the attackers went down. Three more had fallen when the throbbing of the gun abruptly ceased. The magazine was empty!

Mark wiped the palm of his right hand, on his jacket—remembering the bear—and drew the axe, silently cursing himself for neglecting to reload the gun. There was no time now, for he was not at all familiar with the workings of its mechanism.

The Fates must have been chuckling, for as Nona obeyed his command to turn and run again toward the forest, she slipped on the treacherous sand and was immediately grabbed up by a burly golden-haired giant.

The Viking had his hands full, for the now tireless girl fought like a wildcat, squirming and scratching and biting.

But Mark saw none of this, for he was quite busy himself. There were about twenty-six of the rovers, and he was certain he was going to cut this number down considerably before they finally got him. The first to meet him was a bearded giant, fleeter of foot than his companions, for he was several feet in advance.

With a tigerish spring, Mark sunk his axe through the fellow's steel helmet and snatched the short-sword out of his lifeless hand. A wrench tore the axe loose while the sword in his left hand fended off a blow from the next one.

In two heart-beats he was dispatched in a like manner. But now the rest of Mark's attackers had come up and were methodically surrounding him. The cuts he was receiving caused not the slightest pain for they healed as fast as they came.

Time after time the Vikings were about to cut him down

trom the sides and rear, but his flashing sword and shearing axe saved him.

BUT THE inevitable finally happened. A sword blow, delivered from behind, gave his skull a terrific thump. There was a bright flash, a feeling of falling, and then darkness. He was unconscious for only a few minutes, but when he awoke he was trussed up so securely that he could hardly move. A twist of his head revealed that Nona was similarly bound. She didn't look very frightened. Just mad. Mark grinned.

The Norsemen—the ones who weren't dead or sitting on the ground nursing their wounds—were arguing apparently about Mark's stainless-steel axe, held gingerly by a blond Viking who seemed to be their chief.

Their guttural speech was totally unfamiliar to Mark, and the occasional awed glance in his direction from one or another of his captors made even less sense.

After a minute, the chief bent over to examine Mark's wounds. There weren't any. Not even scars. Another discussion arose over this, but it sounded like so much Swedish to Mark. Swedish! That blamed Omega again! He had foreseen that Mark would run afoul of these rovers. And he had evidently known that they would not be killed, but merely taken prisoners.

Finally the Norsemen seemed to have come to some sort of conclusion, for the chief approached and spoke in a respectful tone of voice and motioned for Mark and Nona to rise.

There was a great confusion for a few minutes as the survivors made provision to carry their fallen comrades. Mark noticed with approval that the dead were to be taken along as well as the wounded. This placed his conquerors on a definitely higher plane than his former captors, who had left the dead behind, and killed the wounded rather than be encumbered with them. He suddenly chuckled at the thought that these men were in for a great surprise. Four of the corpses were due to come to life when the effects of the drugged needles wore off.

The presence of Norsemen, fantastic as it might be, meant
that there must be a ship somewhere in the vicinity. Yet there
was none in sight. The question was answered in short order
when the chief led the way around the seaward side of the cliff.
There, standing well off from the shore was a long, low-slung,
single-masted ship, barely visible in the fast-fading twilight.

Evidently the shallow slope of the shore had prevented closer
approach, for the boat lay just outside the whitecaps, rising and
falling with each rolling wave.

Without any hesitation the Norsemen plunged into the sea,
herding Mark and Nona along. Four of the leather-clad giants
took it upon themselves to assist the captives, as the water
deepened and it became increasingly difficult to maintain
balance without the use of their arms.

The two who aided Mark were frankly curious and took this
opportunity to squeeze his biceps and test the hardness of his
abdominal muscles. In fact so attentive were this pair, that,
slightly alarmed, Mark twisted around to see if Nona was being
similarly treated.

In the main, the ship was a typical Viking raiding-vessel.
High-prowed, and equally high in the stern, its sleek lines were
marred by the long row of out-jutting oars. These were out-
rigged to provide a maximum leverage.

The sail, now furled, was a departure from the traditional
Viking style. Its yards and halyards were of an improved rig,
and, Mark guessed, far more manageable than the older type.

As the wading party advanced several more details showed
variance with his recollection of Norse ships. Although his
knowledge might have been gleaned from unreliable sources,
Mark was sure, for one thing, that Viking vessels were not nearly
so large as this one appeared to be. But these were not Vikings
of the tenth century. Of the same general racial stock and possibly a similar state of culture, they must have retained some of
the knowledge that was theirs before the series of wars that
wrecked civilization throughout the world.

WILLING HANDS hauled them aboard. The captives were allowed to stand at the base of the thick mast while the chief disappeared into a cabin in the fore part of the ship. A guttural chattering was going on between those who had remained on board and the landing party. Several times Mark noticed curious stares in his direction and twice as often in Nona's. Her scanty clothing, soaking wet, probably accounted for this. He scowled helplessly.

"What will they do with us?" queried Nona.

Mark looked at her with pride. Her face showed only the calm, unruffled placidity that was her natural expression.

"It's hard to say," he agreed. "But for the present there's no need to worry. The sight of my blue blood, and the way my wounds healed has got them buffaloed. And then too, we both fought like wildcats and if these apes are anything like their ancestors, they have a great admiration and respect for physical valor. Keep your chin up. We'll come out on top."

His words were a lot more cheerful than his thoughts. His recollection of Viking history was far from reassuring. The old Norsemen, as far as he could remember, were not given to going about shedding sweetness and light. They had at one time, in fact, forced the king of France to hand over a large portion of his land. They had raided Paris on several occasions. Very tough people.

The chief reappeared, barking orders. The oars were manned and the big squaresail unfurled. An offshore breeze soon had the craft scudding out to sea, and the oars were no longer needed.

As soon as the ship was well under way, and there was no longer any need for his supervision, the chief addressed Mark with a series of unintelligible gutturals. Then realizing that he was not understood, he beckoned and led the way back to the cabin. To the prisoners' surprise, its interior was as barbarically luxurious as a sultan's seraglio.

On a cushioned divan reclined a rawboned giant with a

flowing white beard and a decidedly emaciated appearance. This ancient had the look of one who was suffering from, or just recovering from, a wasting illness.

By the deferential attitude of the chief Mark wrongly deduced that this old one was the captain of the ship and the other was second in command, acting-chief during his commander's illness. The yellow-haired one gave a stiff bow and made a sort of salute with his right hand and with the same motion waved it toward the captives, as if presenting them.

He then stepped back and effaced himself while the ancient calmly inspected the two prisoners. While so doing, the decrepit old fellow propped himself up on one elbow, and then, after a long minute, sat erect. The look of astonishment on the other Viking's face gave Mark reason to believe that the old fellow hadn't sat up for many a day. He was evidently recovering, then, though just what effect that might have on Nona's and his welfare he had no way of telling.

"Your knife, Sven, son of Sven," quavered the ancient, finally, holding out his hands. The words, of course, were Swedish but their meaning was made clear when the chief produced the knife.

Mark wondered what was coming, but stood quietly waiting, as did Nona. There was nothing they could do, even if the ancient should decide to slide the weapon between their ribs. Mark wondered if his new healing powers would stand up under that kind of punishment. He was afraid not.

But the oldster didn't seem to have anything like that in mind, for with a great creaking of stiffened joints, he rose to his feet and started hacking away at the wet bonds which were cutting into Mark's wrists.

The yellow-haired chief looked on wide-eyed, but made no attempt to interfere. The old man seemed to be quite a guy, Mark decided, for he remembered that Vikings were not inclined to be respectful to anybody who couldn't command their respect.

But then these weren't really Vikings. He mustn't be deceived too much by appearances. They might turn out to be very nice, once he got to know them. Even quite gay characters. The business of the sudden attack on shore didn't necessarily mean anything. It seemed to be the order of the day to attack—or avoid strangers.

He would have to adjust his mind to life in this new world, where only primitive reactions were to be expected. In this age it paid to look on every stranger as an enemy until he proved he wasn't.

THE BONDS parted and Mark flexed his muscles. He was surprised to see that the ancient was holding the knife for him to take.

The chief was equally surprised and this time could not hold his peace, "Don't!" he cried, and moved forward to interfere. "He will kill you!"

But the graybeard waved him aside. "Know you, Sven," he admonished, "that this one is the chosen of Thor, the master of thunder. He is an earthly representative of the Hammer-thrower. Have you not seen proof enough? His influence has already cured my affliction. Observe!"

The ancient squatted and sprang erect several times in quick succession, at the same time flinging his arms wildly about. Not understanding the reason for these calisthenics, the captives wondered vaguely if the oldster wasn't probably a shade unhinged, but Yellow-hair was impressed.

"I bow to your superior knowledge, O Wise One," he said, and did.

Mark, at this point, quickly took the proffered knife before the old fellow could go into his dance again. In an instant Nona was likewise free. Mark returned the knife to the dumbfounded chief.

"I don't know what it's all about," Mark informed Nona, "but it looks as if the danger is over. The old gent seems friendly."

The ancient was looking at the chief triumphantly, having

proved his point. "I shall now," he proclaimed, "speak with the strangers in the language of the Asa, the Gods, which they understand."

Then turning to the prisoners he said: "Ay tank everything bane okay now. Ay tank ve go home."

Mark looked at Nona and Nona looked at Mark. Then they both looked at the ancient. Mark groaned. "Omega! I might have known."

The ancient turned, to the chief, Sven, son of Sven, as if pleased with Mark's words. "The chosen of Thor tells me that he forgives you for attacking him and his mate," he said. "And furthermore that the Valkyrs will bear those that he was forced to kill to their eternal glory in Valhalla. You may tell this to our men. And distribute mead that all may rejoice in the good fortune that is ours in having such guests. Now go and leave us alone."

Sven, with a stiff bow which shook his long hair into his eyes, left the cabin. The ancient grinned impishly, and addressed the captives. "You vars speaking of Omega? Ay nefer bane heard of him."

Mark eyed him askance, far from convinced. When unusual things happened, Omega was very apt to be within haling distance. "I hate to dispute my elders," he mused, aloud. "But that's very corny Svenska you're handing out. Quit playing, will you?"

"Whippersnapper!" raged the spurious Swede. "Can't I have any fun? You'll talk back to the wrong guy some day, and he'll spill some of your aristocratic hemoglobin. Scoffer!"

Still muttering the old man let his aged body creakily down on the cushioned divan. "I ought to do something for this old duffer," the quavering voice resumed, in quieter tones. "After all, he's allowing me the use of his body, even if he does think I am the spirit of Odin." The body stretched and started to fill out before their eyes. Some of the gauntness seemed to leave the face, but it still remained the face of an old man. "Mustn't go too far or they won't recognize him. But this should give him forty years more and he was dying when I took charge."

CHAPTER XII

WHOM THE GODS HAVE CHOSEN

MARK PULLED NONA down on an upholstered bench beside him. "Of course this is none of my business, but would you mind clearing away some of the fog? Don't put yourself out, mind you."

Omega sat up, chuckling. "I get a kick out of watching you two. Not that I sicced these latter-day Vikings on you. I admit I knew you would run into them if you went in the direction I sent you. If I had advised any other course, you would have fared a lot worse.

"Matter of fact I couldn't have prevented that fight by any normal means, but I did save you from having your head sliced off on two occasions. That was one of the reasons that those men were so in awe of you. The two men who swung those blows swore that their axes struck a wall in front of your neck. And that is what started them noticing that, although they had cut you up a good bit, the wounds had healed. After that they were willing to believe anything."

"Thanks. But here we are, in the middle of the ocean headed for Iceland, or some such place. What's the idea? A bit of a warning, since you were watching us anyway, and we might have avoided all this."

"What's the difference? What was formerly your country is now just so much territory overrun by savage tribes, here and there dotted with cities in a more or less feudal state. There is no more civilization there than there is anywhere else in the world.

"These Vikings are just as advanced as any race on the face of the Earth. And as far as social relations are concerned, they come closer to the old American traditions than any of the other races. They value personal independence highly, and look with suspicion on anyone who tries to govern them with an iron hand. They work together under a leader only when that leader has proven himself capable. No four-flusher can make them follow like a bunch of sheep.

"Taking it all in all they're not such a benighted race, even if they do like a spot of pillage once in a while. That comes mainly under the head of exuberant animal spirits. They're not essentially cruel."

"That may be true, but now we'll have to learn a new language, and be governed according to the customs of these people, or else leave them and make a home for ourselves in some totally unfamiliar land."

"Use your head, son. After six thousand years, don't you think the topography of the land is changed as well as the people? America is not as you left it. There are mountains where you knew valleys; lakes where there was land. For instance, you struck a path today aimed to bring you to the seashore about opposite the tip of Long Island. It didn't, for the place no longer exists. Long Island gradually sank until now it is below sea level. It was gone for years before anyone noticed.

"And as far as customs are concerned, you certainly wouldn't want to live out your lives as complete hermits. You'd have to conform to the customs of some race. And among these people you will be big-shots. Chosen of the gods! I fixed that for you. You'll have to prove it every so often, for these lads don't take much on hearsay, but you can do that easily."

Mark looked at Nona, who was keeping a discreet silence. She seemed perfectly happy just to sit beside him and listen.

"I don't want to give the impression of seeming ungrateful," Mark said. "We both appreciate the things you have done—

barring the practical jokes—but I don't fancy this business of sailing under false colors. Chosen of the gods!"

"**I EXPECTED** you to pull that. Now listen.... If I had given any other explanation for your physical peculiarities, they might not even have let you live. And if they had, you could never have associated with them on an even footing. You would have been a pariah, something not altogether to be trusted. An Elk at a Shriner's clambake....

"On the other hand, if you are considered a sort of demigod blessed by their most respected deity, Thor, they will envy and respect you, but nevertheless treat you as one of them. It's the type of thing they would fall for, too. They believe their gods are very close to them and interested in their slightest actions. Every exploit of theirs succeeds or fails only because the god interested approves or disapproves.

"And think of Nona. Her chances of safety are improved immensely."

Mark made a helpless gesture.

"I shouldn't have started this discussion in the first place," he growled. "There seems to be nothing to do but begin taking lessons in Swedish."

"It's not exactly Swedish. It's a conglomeration of three or four languages—Swedish, Norwegian, Danish and several dialects—all of them changed considerably by the passage of time. But I'll spare you the mental effort of learning it."

He arose, placed a hand on Mark's head and stared into his eyes.

For the first time it was driven home to Mark the terrific mind-energy that was Omega's. The impact of irresistible thought waves made his brain reel. It seemed as if a hammer was beating repeatedly—throbbingly—inside his skull. His senses were dimming and he had almost lapsed into unconsciousness when Omega quit and moved over to Nona. Mark shook his head several times, trying to clear it and gain sufficient possession of his faculties to stop Omega from subjecting Nona to the torture he had just endured. But the operation was completed before he could speak.

"Calm yourself," said the ancient, in the Viking language, which Mark realized he could now understand as well as English, "I deadened her brain before I forced the change in her memory cells. She felt no pain. I'd have done the same for you except that you needed taking down a peg or two."

"I'm chastened. But the next time I'll learn languages in the ordinary manner."

"I'll have to explain to Sven that your keenness of mind—a gift conferred by Thor—enabled me to teach you the tongue in short order." Omega chuckled.

"Now suppose you two adjourn to the next room until daylight. I have some thinking to do."

CHAPTER XIII

MARK, THE MIGHTY

MORNING FOUND THE ship well out of sight of land, scudding with shortened sail before a fresh west wind. The sky was cloudless and the sun was so low on the horizon when Mark first set foot on the deck, that it seemed the ship was sailing directly into it.

Omega had brought out an assortment of feminine apparel for Nona to select from. The clothing was some of the loot garnered from one of the cities further south on the American coast, and consisted of the same sort of barbaric costumes as the one she had been wearing. There was variety, of course, but none of the outfits would have been suitable in a nunnery.

Omega had also provided a change for Mark, a Viking costume more in keeping with his surroundings. The shiny axe, which had been the center of the Norse-men's discussion, had been returned and was now swinging from his belt on the right side, while on the left was a shortsword of excellent manufacture, a gift from Sven.

Nona had elected to stay in the cabin, which was to be theirs for the duration of the journey, and do a bit of tidying up. There were furnishings to be rearranged, she explained; and he might as well run along and get acquainted with the crew until she finished, or he would get in her way. So Mark was alone as he squinted into the rays of the rising sun. Sven had seen him emerge and was approaching from amidships. At the same time the door at his elbow opened and the ancient priest housing Omega's mind-stepped forth.

"Thought I had better remind you about proving your standing with Thor. You can't back down now, you know. That would make a liar out of the old guy whose body I'm using."

"Old guy! What's that make you?... Tell me what to do, before Sven gets here."

"Well, Thor is supposed to be a great hand at throwing the hammer. You might try that."

"You know darn well I couldn't hit the side of the Empire State Building with a hammer."

"No? Well, use your axe then. In a minute I'm going to tell Sven to clear the deck for an axe-throwing exhibition, so you had better be good."

Mark's throat rumbled, but Sven had arrived, so he kept still. The Viking brought up his arm in the salute he had used the night before. This time it seemed to include both of them. Mark decided to return it. This man was the captain of the ship, he had learned; the real leader of the expedition. An attempt to win his friendship seemed to be wise. Omega didn't do likewise, for, playing the part of the wise old man, it wouldn't be in character. The ancient was on board, as he had explained earlier in the morning, in the capacity of an advisor and medical man. His position commanded respect mainly because of his own wisdom and age. He had no real authority in an active sense, but was nevertheless consulted before any major step was taken.

Sven seemed to be quite pleased that Mark had returned his salute.

"My men greet you," be said, "and wish to state that they are gratified that you hold no malice because of our attack yesterday. Those who survived appreciate that they are alive today only because you allowed yourself to be captured rather than take the lives of any more brave men. They also asked me to extend their regret at ignorantly having laid hands on your mate."

Mark rallied quickly. "You may say to your men that their actions were only natural and to think no more of the affair. It is forgotten."

Sven bowed with the stiff inclination of the head that was characteristic. "There is something—the men would like explained, if it is not too presumptuous. Two of my men attest to the fact that when they aimed a blow which should have cut off your head, their axes rebounded as if striking a wall. Was this imagination, or what?"

Mark smiled enigmatically. "That is hard to answer," he said, quite frankly. "But there is every chance that my patron interposed an obstacle in front of the axes. It has happened before. I remember once…. But then that was different. There was a bear and I had the axe. No, that was different. But as I said, you can blame it on my patron. He is notoriously inclined to do strange and wondrous things."

MARK WAS looking at Omega, who furtively looked back through the fingers of a hand placed before his face. But suddenly he snapped the hand down and addressed Sven.

"Our honored guest," he announced pompously, "has consented to put the minds of our men at ease, in case they are secretly ashamed of the fact that they were not able to conquer him without such terrific loss. He is going to show that, due to the skill with which he has been endowed by his patron, Thor, no small body of warriors could hope to prevail over him. You will prepare a space for the throwing of the axe."

And suddenly there was a living wall in front of them—a wall of yelling, charging Mongols.

Sven turned on his heel and set out to clear the deck.

"Now you've done it!" Mark growled. "I wish I could throw an axe as well as you throw the bull."

Omega regarded him with a twinkle in his eyes. "I think I'll give you another language lesson," he said. "Or maybe you would learn to be more respectful to your elders if I gave you a complete knowledge and understanding of the various Einstein concepts. All in one quick dose!"

Mark winced. "I'll behave," he promised. "But I still can't throw an axe; not with any remarkable degree of accuracy."

"What are you worrying about? You have a splendid physique. The necessary muscles are well developed. All you do is aim the axe at the target and heave with all your strength. Simple! Of course I'll be on the sidelines, rooting."

"That ought to be a great help. But the point is, will it? You're such a great practical joker. It won't surprise me if the axe lands in the sea."

Sven had gone efficiently about his task. Every man on board, with the exception of the helmsman, who luckily had a clear view of the deck, was lined up against the rails to watch the performance.

Omega led the way to a point about seventy-five feet from the mast, and held up his hands for silence.

"Our distinguished guest, Mark, the axe-thrower, has consented to give you an exhibition of his skill. He requests a volunteer."

A chorus of yells indicated that there were plenty of takers. Sven was among them. He was directed to stand a few feet away from the mast. Omega produced a twig, about a foot long, and placed it in the volunteer's mouth.

Mark's heart sank. It was his job to knock it out, and yet he knew that he would have to have assistance or the Vikings would soon be voting for a new captain. With a silent prayer he firmly gripped the axe and measured the distance with a deliberate eye. Corded muscles stood out in relief as he slowly drew back his arm.

Then, with the speed of a striking snake, the arm shot out, releasing the axe.

With a swish that could be heard all over the deck, the axe cleaved the air, speeding true to its mark. The twig was sheared off close to Sven's lips. But the axe did not spend its force by falling to the deck. Oh no. Not with Omega directing the performance. It continued flying, described an arc around the thick mast and sped back to Mark! Fortunately he saw it coming and caught it, calmly restoring it to his belt.

For an instant there was a dead silence, while Sven removed the short piece of twig from his mouth and gazed at it stupidly. Then bedlam broke loose.

Someone picked up the broken bit of twig and the men fought each other for a look at it. Some crowded about Mark and Omega and respectfully asked for a closer inspection of the axe. Its keen edge and stainless steel surface hypnotized them. Surely this axe was forged by the gods! No other answer could explain its quality or ability. No other weapon known to them would return to the hand of the thrower. It was evident that the men who had not witnessed the fight on shore were just as convinced as the others of Mark's divine guidance. Only the hammer of Thor could perform that trick.

BACK IN the cabin Nona heard about the performance. Mark spoke apologetically, embarrassed by the deception, but Omega was chuckling gleefully.

"You'll simply have to get over your squeamishness," he told Mark. "We've really done them a favor. Given them something new and wonderful to talk about. And in a way, we've shown them the power of their gods. I've found that's always a comfort to mortals."

"More trickery," Mark commented.

Omega looked surprised. "About the gods? Not at all. You know, that's one reason why I've always been interested in humans. They must have something to worship. I used to think it was plain ignorance of natural phenomena that caused them to explain everything they didn't understand by devising beings with supernatural powers. But surely, if that was the reason, there would be somewhere a group of humans who would explain things that they could not understand by admitting they had not yet gained sufficient knowledge. But there has never in the history of mankind been a race of people who did not have some sort of deity—"

"I know," agreed Mark. "And the logical inference is: Fifty billion humans can't be wrong. There *must* be a deity."

"Nonsense, my superstitious idiot. Among humans, majorities have always been wrong, and you know it. Cite one instance where a majority has been right. I dare you!"

Mark thought for a minute. "There must be one somewhere…."

"There isn't. That is why man is where he is today. Majorities rule and majorities are always wrong. The multitude always allows itself to be swayed by some loudmouth who promises a lot, but who really holds his own interests paramount.

"Now, now.... I'll admit there have been some really selfless men who did manage to get a following. Confucius, Christ, a few others.... But the reason they ultimately failed lay not in their lack of merit, but in the crass stupidity of those they tried to help. A race who, in a fevered instant, could forget all the benevolent teachings pounded into them for generations, and foolishly follow a madman into war. I don't know why somebody hasn't destroyed the race long ago. If it wasn't against my principles I would have done it myself."

"Could you do it?" asked Mark, curious.

"Certainly. In an hour your whole atmosphere could be ionized. That would do the job nicely." Omega looked about, calculatingly; and for a moment a look came into his eyes that made Mark extremely apprehensive. It was the look of a man to whom world-cataclysm would be not only possible but even desirable.

"But no one would take the trouble to destroy the world, of course. Why should they?" Mark put in quickly. He was relieved to see the look fade from Omega's eyes.

"I really don't know," Omega informed him. "I'm derelict in my duty for not doing it myself. For some day a civilization will develop to reach the point in scientific advancement where space can be conquered. And when man does that, he will colonize. The specked apple in the barrel of life will then contaminate the universe. To the detriment of worthier civilizations. Some entity with the power to manipulate cosmic forces, such as myself, will then be obliged to take action to protect other forms of life-forms which have not been instilled with the desire to exterminate and kill wantonly, as humans are wont to do. When that day comes the rotten apple will be tossed out of the barrel."

"Meaning humanity," murmured Mark, a bit worried. "Something will have to be done about it."

"I've already done it."

"You don't say?"

"Sure, I told you about it. This new race I've created in the persons of you and Nona."

"YOU DIDN'T create Nona and me. You just woke me up, as any alarm clock could have done; and you gave Nona an injection which could have been done by the old doc, if he had been alive. Don't take on such airs. Created us—bah!

Omega took that amiably.

"All right, get technical, you cub. The idea was mine, anyway. What I started to say was that in you and Nona we have two people who have the more admirable qualities in dominance. Your offspring will inherit the tendency. And due to the fact that your descendants will be long-lived, scientific and social progress will be much faster than with the short-lived race of normal humans.

"The ability and power of a brain increases with age, provided it is not being poisoned by an aging body. With the new race the individual will live long enough to utilize the learning that he acquires. The ordinary human begins to decline long before his accumulated knowledge can be put to any useful purpose.

"Here and there have been men energetic enough to accomplish a few triumphs before this decay set in, but they have been few and far between. Usually a man dies before his brain develops sufficiently for him to understand the most elementary of natural phenomena. And that, no doubt, explains why he fortifies himself with a belief in the supernatural, knowing subconsciously that he can never hope to solve the mysteries of the universe."

"And that brings us back to religion. How'd we ever come to get off it?"

Omega glared in a ferocious manner. "My fault, moron. I forgot to keep my streamlined intellect on a narrow-gauge rail."

Mark grinned.

"How you do run on. Scrambling similes and mixing meta-phors. From rotten apples to railroads."

Nona, at this point, indicated that she was still with them. "I think it was very wise to get off the subject of religion," she said. "From my readings it would appear that whenever people argue about religion they become bad friends. And the argument never accomplishes anything, anyway. Each goes away believing just as he always believed, except that he now thinks less of the other. Then too, the whole thing is of little importance, for there have always been devils who went to church and angels who didn't. What you believe isn't nearly so important as how you use what you do believe."

Mark and Omega looked at each other. Neither spoke for a moment, and both knew the sheepishness men feel when a mere woman puts a simple end-mark to a complicated and sterile masculine harangue.

"There might be something in what she says," Mark, deflated, admitted.

CHAPTER XIV

HARBOR OF WOMEN

CROSSING THE ATLANTIC in a Viking ship turned out to be a long drawn out process. When the wind failed the vessel was propelled by oars, but the speed was agonizingly snail-like.

As the journey wore on, Mark found himself liking more and more the hardy crew. Sven, particularly, he found to be congenial company. And, as Omega had predicted, the Norsemen came to accept him as one of them, without any reservation on the score of his peculiar talents. That they were associating with a man who had been singled out to be favored with special gifts from a god, was a matter of course. Such things had happened before, had, they not? It was just their good luck to meet up with one so favored.

Several times during the journey the disturbing recollection of Omega's story of the two Russians, came to plague Mark during the long night hours when he was trying to sleep.

Peculiar thing, this sleep business. Omega had assured him that although he really didn't require sleep with his new blood, he would nevertheless find himself able to whenever he wished. The explanation had something to do with habit, and the fact that the race had been accustomed to sleeping a certain percentage of the day.

The idea may have been very sound, and it certainly did apply in Nona's case, but Mark, who had always been an insomniac, found that the theory did not work out in practice.

There were times, of course, when he did manage to compose his thoughts and woo the elusive somnolent state, but far more often he would find his mind racing away to cope with imaginary problems, or perhaps to review some incident in his past and deciding how he would act if the episode were to be lived over.

At such times he would curse his inability to control his mind, and would try mightily to lead his thoughts to calmer channels. This, naturally, would make him even more wide-awake, and he would give up and go outside to pace the deck or talk to the crew. This increased his knowledge of the manners and customs of the Vikings, and due to his willingness to listen and learn, he always found an eager tutor.

Occasionally he would take part in a wrestling match with one of the crew. This was a popular sport among the Norsemen, who admired strength greatly. In fact it was his ability at this pastime which accounted mainly for his rise in popularity. For at one time or another he defeated every man on board. This was not due to any great skill or superior knowledge of the art, but rather to the fact that he was tireless.

Whenever he found himself clamped in a hold beyond his ability to break, he would just relax and wait for his opponent to tire. And even with his most powerful adversary this was sure to happen, for it takes a lot of energy to maintain a punishing hold. And when the Norseman had tired sufficiently Mark would proceed to pin his shoulders to the mat.

But eventually his companionship with the crew grew tiresome. He learned all he could from them, and they certainly were not brilliant conversationalists. Their stories of past exploits were entertaining but they all began to sound alike. And so he would spend nights in his cabin where Nona was sleeping as peacefully as a baby, and think. And he was surprised how logical and coherent his thought processes became with practice.

He realized that he had really never thought before. Now he found that he not only was cerebrating abstractly, but enjoying it. Here was another side of the coin Omega had paid out when he spoke of the quicker progress that should be made by a race of men with Mark's characteristics.

THE AVERAGE human spent the greater portion of his day working to keep his stomach full, and the better part of the night sleeping. All this time was free to the man with Mark's peculiar attributes, and it followed that even in an ordinary lifetime much greater progress could be made in the matter of mental development. If only he could control those vagrant thoughts that insisted upon troubling him, those nights would be a pleasure. He began to consider the two Russians Omega had told him about. Brains equal in capacity to the mighty mind of Omega, yet twisted so that human suffering meant nothing compared with the enjoyment of seeing some experiment work itself out.

These minds were a constant menace to any progressive civilization. It might even be that they would refuse to allow any advanced civilization ever to develop. It seemed likely that such minds would take steps to prevent the development of other brains that might at some future date challenge their right to ride rough-shod over the rights of others. Here was a problem that some day must be faced. And the future of his own descendants was at stake, for the Russians, when they finally returned to their earthly habitation, would be quick to see the possibilities of this new race.

Yet it seemed hopeless to try to figure any way of combating a danger that Omega admitted was too much for him.

Several times, however, he felt he had almost caught the answer. But whenever this happened, some fleeting idea on an entirely unrelated theme would break his train of thought. It was exasperating; he would try for hours to recapture the sequence of thought which had led to that almost-point, only to fail and give up in disgust. On such occasions he would be irritable for hours afterward; Nona was very patient with him then, and he loved her more than ever.

That elusive train of thought always started with the doubt that the Russians were as powerful as Omega believed. He had Omega's word that the ability of a brain increased with age. And certainly he was immeasurably older than the comparatively youthful composite Russian brains.

From that premise the thought followed that in all probability the Russians had not nearly the control over the forces of nature that Omega had. They would be, after a mere four thousand years, and having sprung from an intellectually inferior race, only tyros in the use of their powers. It was possible that they were accomplishing their ends by forcing their wills through hypnotism on the peoples with whom they experimented. This, he realized, would be a juvenile method to Omega. A child's meaningless trick.

But there the train of thought always ended. He could never co-relate these deductions to any logical conclusion. No plan of action resulted. Sometimes he would carry the matter further than others, but always he would wind up against a stone wall. The reason for it probably lay in the fact that these thoughts of the Russians always crept in at a time when he was concentrating on some other subject. And his mind, not yet as capable as it was later to become, would veer back to the original train of thought, leaving him worse off than when he started.

For he would realize that as he tried to continue one he had lost the other. And the realization angered him. It seemed that no matter how brilliantly his mind functioned during these long, quiet nights, there was always this business of the Russians to annoy him. Sooner or later he would have to settle the thing or he would be receiving his mail in some Viking psychopathic ward.

OMEGA, WHO was staying with them for some reason that Mark was not able to fathom, noticed the periods of ill-humor, but refrained from remarking upon them. Mark often wondered whether his mind was being probed without his knowledge, but Omega had never given any indication that he did this. It was possible that Omega was staying because he realized what was troubling Mark and wanted to see just how he would manage to solve the problem.

The voyage was coming to the close of its third month when a lookout in the rigging announced that land was in sight. Excitement ran high among the Norsemen until it was determined just what land it was. Their navigation instruments were pretty inaccurate, Mark discovered, and a captain who hit land less than two or three hundred miles from his port was considered a distinctly superior seaman. This time, however, it quickly determined that they were heading directly toward the home port, a point on the coast of Norway once known as Stadtland.

Mark looked knowingly at Omega, for it was obvious that all the others were very much surprised at this unusual navigation. Sven seemed to be very puffed up about the whole thing.

Omega grinned. "We were headed for the coast of Spain until I made a few corrections," he admitted to Mark. "It's a miracle these lads ever get anywhere. Their seamanship is more to nerve than brains. I feel sorry for them, now, though. They don't know what is in store for them."

Mark was alarmed. "What's wrong?"

"You'll find out when we land." Beyond that Omega would say nothing.

The sail was furled as the ship approached the little cove that comprised the harbor. People had gathered on shore to welcome them; and beyond were the solid-looking houses of a small town. Further in the background was a stone structure, something on the order of a medieval castle, but smaller.

"There don't seem to be many on shore," remarked Sven, peering under his shading hand. "They appear to be mostly women. By the Aesir, they are *all* women! Have we become outcasts that we should be greeted by women?"

His voice was angry.

There were echoing growls from others among the crew, but the men were too glad to be home to be upset by such a minor matter. Probably their king had organized a large hunt and the men were all away. The crowd was swelling in size, but there were still nothing but women. And they watched silently. No cheer went up. No hand waved. No mouth smiled.

CHAPTER XV

SOLDIERS—TO WAR!

UNDER THE DRIVE of many oars the vessel soon was beached. With shouts, the Norsemen leaped into the shallow water and waded ashore. Sven helped the ancient over the side and then waded on ahead. Mark was looking ahead at the first of the Norsemen to arrive on land. He guessed that bad news awaited them and he wondered how bad it would be. The men's glad shouts died out as more and more of them reached the crowd on the beach. Sven had already talked to one of the women and waded part-way out again. Then he stopped, passed a hand before his face, and stood silent and bewildered.

"What is it, Sven?" Mark demanded, gripping his arm.

The giant looked up blankly, then shook his head. "My father—my sons—dead!" he mumbled. "Dead—and my boy Sven would soon have been a man."

The story his bereaved wife had told him came stumbling from his lips.

Only a month before, the town had been attacked by strange nomads. The defenders fought with the fury of demons; but the invaders kept coming in countless thousands and at last overwhelmed them. Every townsman was slaughtered, and when no more resistance was forthcoming the horde entered the homes and killed all the boys, even to the tiniest baby. No girls or women were even molested. After their mission had been accomplished the invaders marched away and disappeared into the forest.

The following days had been busy ones for the surviving women, who were left with the task of burying their dead. With relief they had greeted the arrival of two shiploads of returning seamen a week after the catastrophe. But on the following day the invaders had reappeared and massacred these, again leaving a town bereft of men. Now the women were entreating these new arrivals to leave, lest they too, lose their lives. And their wives, mothers and daughters were begging to leave with them.

Sven turned to Omega and asked for advice, but Mark interrupted. "Have the ship provisioned immediately. We set sail as soon as it can be done."

Sven looked his astonishment. "But we can't leave the women. Suppose the invaders return?"

"Could you do anything if they did? I am offering the only possible chance for revenge and freedom from another attack. Order the ship provisioned. It's all right, Sven. I have a plan."

Sven, still bewildered, looked to Omega for guidance. A nod answered him, and Sven set about his task with a flurry of activity. The whys and wherefores were not important as long as he had something to occupy his hands, his muscles.

"You've guessed the answer, eh?" inquired Omega.

"Part of it. You'll have to supply the rest. Where are they?"

"Do you mean their egos, or their brains?"

"The brains, of course."

"The place is not far from Arkhangelsk, on the White Sea. The spot was chosen originally because it was removed from civilization. And the brains remain there for the same reason, though they could move if they wished. But how did you guess it was they?"

"You said they enjoyed pitting one community against another in conflict, and watching the fight as if it were a football game. And you said they like to experiment and dabble in the lives of different peoples and watch the results of their meddling. The deduction is therefore that they threw this band of invaders—probably creations of their own, judging by their numbers, and the fact that they left the women alone—into action, just to watch the fight, and with the added purpose of finding how a community of women would fare without men. Nice chaps. Right?"

"Right. But I didn't expect you to figure it out so quickly. You must have got another brain cell, working during those nights you didn't manage to sleep."

Mark grinned. "Yes. I have two now."

THE WORK of refitting the ship went on quickly. Women, with pathetically hopeless expressions on their faces, carried preserved foods down to the shore, and helped every way they could. Most of them had already lost their menfolk. Others were just as anxiously helping to get their men, members of this crew, away before the invaders returned to kill them. This group was not so hopeless, for Mark had allowed Sven to tell them that they had a plan to forestall the invaders, and that their men would return. He wasn't at all certain that he could keep this heroic promise, but it did no harm to give these forlorn women a little crumb of hope.

There was another group in the town—quite a sizable one—comprising the women whose husbands and sons were still at sea. These still clung to their courage, for there was the chance that by the time their men did return, Sven's crew would have already conquered the invaders, just what plan could expect to prevail against such a vast horde, no one could guess, but the very fact that there was any kind of a plan, heartened them.

The sun still hovered above the horizon, bathing the western sea with a reddish glow, when the ship again put to sea. This journey was to be a long journey, over a thousand miles of coastwise travel, but Omega winked at Mark when he mentioned that fact. "Be of good cheer, my friend," he encouraged, "These fellows have never made any trips in this direction; and so they won't even know it when I shorten the journey by a few hundred miles."

"And how will you go about that?"

"Simple, my doubting friend, simple. Tonight, after most of the men have gone to sleep, I shall cause those on watch to become drowsy, and while they are catching their forty winks, I'll just lift the ship and then set it down within a couple days' radius of the White Sea. They won't know anything happened."

"Simple," repeated Mark. "With all the miracles you can perform I can't see why you haven't exterminated those Russian vermin long ago."

"But I've told you that it is against my principles to do that sort of thing. And besides I'm not at all sure I wouldn't wind up on the wrong end of the exterminating. But you are different. For you, this is a matter of self-preservation. How you intend to do it is beyond me. They could blast you out of existence in an instant."

Mark was silent. "I'm not so sure myself. But I think I have a chance. I'm banking on two things I've learned about them. They do not as yet know that they can exist as pure thought-patterns, without their brains. And they have an overwhelming curiosity."

Omega pondered, and seemed to get nowhere. Mark guessed this to be mere acting, for that was a secret delight of Omega's.

But it might be that the other really had failed to divine his plan. Perhaps Omega really felt himself to be unable to cope with the two Russian brains, and had therefore neglected to consider the direct course that Mark had in mind.

"You wouldn't care to elucidate?" inquired Omega, hopefully.

"No. I have an idea that here is one time when an earthly brain is not wholly inadequate."

"Such conceit! First idea you ever had—probably no good, at that—and now you're getting cocky."

OMEGA OBLIGINGLY performed his navigational miracle after the ship's company had gone to sleep. At Mark's question he explained that his reason for not transporting the ship in this manner with the Norsemen's knowledge was that it wouldn't be good for them to see such weird happenings. Mark's unusual characteristics, however, were well within their scope of understanding. A man could conceivably, by reason of his courage or some other worthy attribute, become a favorite of some god. But for a ship to be lifted through the air would upset them terribly.

The moon was riding high overhead, bathing the waves with a flickering silver light and barely illuminating the distant shoreline, when Omega went to work. The helmsman, dreaming of Valhalla, failed to notice that the wheel no longer tugged at his arms. The few deckhands on duty never knew that for a space of several minutes the creakings and groanings of straining timbers quieted as the ship lifted and was no longer buffeted by wind and wave.

But Mark and Nona, hand in hand, marveled as the craft soared and the waves slid beneath them with astonishing rapidity.

The shoreline became an indistinguishable blur as their speed increased. Even the moon noticeably changed its position. Yet there was no sensation of speed; no raging wind tore the sail to shreds and felled the great mast. This, Omega explained, was

because the surrounding air was traveling with them, enclosed
with the ship inside a globular field of force, created by changing slightly the rays of subcosmic energy which pervades all
space. These rays, he further explained, were waiting to be
tapped by anyone who knew how, and were available anywhere,
for their penetrating power was far superior to that of ordinary
cosmic rays, which became very weak on the surface of a planet
possessing an atmosphere.

Nona shivered a little as the speed decreased and the ship
settled gently into the water. She clung tighter to Mark's arm.

"Cold?" he inquired.

"Scared," she said. "We're almost there, Mark. Oh, Mark....
Let's give it up! We're risking a lifetime of happiness. *Our
lifetime.* We could go to some other part of the world and live
out our lives in peace. This isn't our fight, Mark dear."

Mark didn't answer right away. Then he shook his head and
gave her hand a reassuring pat. "We have to do this, Nona. It
is our fight. There could never be any happiness for us knowing
that this menace is hanging over our heads. Distance wouldn't
save us from them. No matter where we went they could find
us—and fear us. And strike us down. Even if we should live
out our lives undiscovered, we would know that sooner or later
they would find our children and destroy them. No, we couldn't
be happy knowing that."

Nona smiled bravely; but a tear found its way down her
cheek. "You're right of course. This is a good fight, Mark. I know
that. Only do—do please be careful.... I love you so terribly."

"Poor helpless creature," Mark said, grandly. "How I wish I
might love you in return." She pinched his arm savagely. He
yelped.

Omega was regarding them with a wry grin. "Heroics!" he
snorted. "But just the same, you have plenty to worry about.
Those Russians are not nice boys to monkey with. But that's
your worry. I have more important things to think of. I'm going
to leave you now...."

Mark was astonished. "Wait a minute, you wretched little coward. You started this, you know—you might at least hang around while I finish it. How am I ever to manage to find—them?"

"Won't be hard. In the morning you will sight the mouth of the White Sea. Follow the eastern coast until you come to the ruins of the city of Arkhangelsk—yes, there are still some ruins visible, mainly because vegetation doesn't flourish so well in these parts—then continue for about five miles. The coast takes a turn toward the west after you pass the city. Land when you sight a deep ravine, then follow it until you arrive at your destination."

"But how will I know? What's the place look like?"

"You'll know when you get there. Good bye."

WITH A sigh the gaunt figure of the ancient slumped and sat wearily down on a coil of rope. The original owner of the body was now in possession and evidently was bewildered. After a minute he shook his head slowly and looked up.

To Mark and Nona it was the face of a stranger who somnolently regarded them. It was the same cadaverous visage, with the same shock of white hair and snowy beard, but somehow different.

The difference, they realized, was one of expression. Gone was the look of intelligence, the twinkle that mirrored a colossal humor. There was still an illusion of wisdom, but only such wisdom as might be expected of an aged savage, steeped in the lore of a long lifetime. But steeped also in superstition.

"Great indeed are the gods!" he intoned, stumbling to his feet and heading toward his cabin. As he went they could hear him muttering: "Omega or Odin.... What difference? A change of name but not of identity. There can be but one Odin!"

It was a saddened, almost disheartened, pair who followed to the cabin.

"I really shouldn't have expected him to stay," Mark admitted. "I knew he didn't like the job. But somehow I had come to expect that he would be there in the pinches, lending moral support, if nothing else."

"Maybe," Nona hesitated, and then apparently decided to hold her peace.

But Mark divined her thought. "Nothing doing. I'm going through with it anyhow. His absence makes no difference. He didn't figure this out in the first place."

"But you're disappointed."

"Of course I am. But I realize it's not fair. After all, he merely has left me to fight my own battles. This business can have no more than an academic interest for him. And an academic interest is hardly sufficient reason to risk one's life, is it?"

Nona looked at him with adoring eyes. "You're defending him. Yet if the positions were reversed you would have stuck to the bitter end. You thought him a friend."

Mark was silent. You might call it intuition, but it sounded to him altogether too much like cold logic for him to venture any more meaningless argument. He was disappointed, and had to admit it.

Morning came, clear and cold. The course was now southeast, and the shoreline was dimly discernible from starboard. They were now entering the White Sea, really an over-sized bay.

Before long the opposite coast would be visible, and they would follow its contours southward. During all these changes of direction, from northeast to east, to southeast, and finally to south, Mark noticed that the wind blew the ship continually before it, the most advantageous direction for a single square-sail.

It almost looked like one of the devious machinations of Omega. But no…. Omega was gone and it was better not to think of him. He had done wonders for them already and the best thing was to be grateful for favors done rather than bitter at others undone. The favoring wind was merely a stroke of good fortune.

AS YET Mark had said nothing to Sven or any of the crew

explaining the purpose of this voyage. And when he tried to think of words to tell them what they were up against, it seemed best to let the whole matter drop.

He could picture their incredulity if he should even try to tell them of the Russians and how they came to be. The thing was beyond them. He could explain by calling this expedition a crusade against malignant gods, and would be believed. But this went against the grain. He had preyed on their superstitious beliefs too much already.

But the Norsemen seemed willing to follow him without question. The fact that he knew more than they, and had a plan of action appeared to be enough for them. They went about with a grim air, obviously looking forward to some engagement in which they could avenge their lost sons and brothers and insure security for their people.

Mark remembered that he had promised them that, and felt a qualm that he might not be able to deliver when the time came. But if he failed, it would be with the knowledge that no one else would have done better when even Omega had shied clear of the undertaking.

The day was nearing its end when Mark spotted the crumbling ruins of Arkhangelsk. From that point on it was necessary to give strict attention to the shore. He posted men in the rigging as lookouts, for if the ravine described by Omega was missed in the fading light, they might have to spend half the next day retracing their course. His precaution turned out to be unnecessary. The ravine was so deeply cut that it was plainly visible from the deck.

There seemed to be nothing to do now but lie at anchor until morning. For although he was ready to disembark and follow the ravine immediately, the Vikings needed a night's rest. It was probably better that way, anyhow, for he had no idea what lay before them, no idea what the place he sought even looked like. And it would certainly be easier to find it in daylight.

So he spent the night perfecting his plans. Nona stayed awake and occasionally—when he wasn't busy thinking—spoke to him. She harbored a gnawing fear that they were spending their last moments together, but resolutely kept from letting him know it.

Mark had already decided that only half the ship's company was to accompany him. Nona had fussed a good deal about coming along, but Mark wouldn't listen. "Men!" she mumbled irritably and turned away pouting.

Mark had some inkling of the perverse inclinations of the two monster-brains, and he knew how easily they could divert him from his purpose if Nona was along to divide his attention. About thirty-five men would be sufficient to manage the return voyage and warn the survivors in the town of their failure, if failure it was. And the other half would be more than enough to carry out his plan. To take more might mean a needless sacrifice.

Those to remain would be instructed to wait for two days— he had to make it that long, for he had no idea how far his quest might lead him—and then return and warn the townspeople that it would be best to leave the vicinity against the possible return of the invaders. There would be dissension, he knew, when he told the men that only half were to be given a chance for revenge, but he counted on their allegiance to him as a favored one of Thor, to see him through.

Nona put her head against his chest. "I'm sorry I was cross," she whispered. "And please—please do come back—"

CHAPTER XVI

NOMADS AND A DRAGON

THE RAVINE WOUND circuitously toward the interior, and the rocky stubble which littered the ground made traveling difficult. In some distant age in the past, a fast-flowing stream had made this deep cut, strewing rocks and shale haphazardly along its bed.

So early had been their start that the party had covered several miles before the light of the sun was able to light their path. Mark noticed as they traveled, the ravine widened out and flattened.

Noon passed, still without sign that they were nearing their destination.

His companions munched the dried meats they had brought. Mark was glad he had ordered the ship to remain two days, and was wishing he had made it three. But there had been nothing in Omega's instructions to lead him to believe the trip would be very long. Well, there was nothing to do now but push on. And if the round trip took more than two days, they could always cut across land to the Scandinavian peninsula. With luck they might arrive before the ship, which would have a much longer trip, contrary winds, and no help from Omega.

His reverie was shattered by a loud shout from one of the Norsemen. All eyes were following his outstretched hand. Coming toward them at a rapid trot were more than a score of horsemen!

Mark gasped. For these horsemen were relics of an age long dead before his birth. They were nomads such as those who rode and ravaged under the leadership of Il Khan, the Mongol chief. Conical hats, *yataghans* and nondescript mounts, there could be no mistaking the rovers, though their period of existence had lapsed many thousands of years past.

Yelling orders, he deployed his men in a long line against the nearest wall of the ravine. This move canceled any advantage the enemy's horses might give them. Without any apparent plan the horsemen spread and charged. But the charge lost its force when the wall made them slow up their mounts to prevent dashing themselves to pieces against its sides. With a timing that could not have been better had it been rehearsed, each Norseman picked his adversary and attacked at the moment when the horse was partially out of control due to the change in pace.

Several *yataghans* found sheaths in Viking flesh in that instant of wild fighting, but the result was never in doubt.

Nomad after slant-eyed nomad was dragged from his horse and cut down by axes which seemed imbued with a desire for vengeance all their own. In a few minutes the battle was over.

The riderless horses were fleeing back in the direction where they had come from, and the Vikings were reckoning their losses.

The Norsemen suffered four casualties. Two would never fight again, and the other two had been bandaged and left in the ravine to be helped back to the ship when the party returned.

MARK WAS puzzled by a strange phenomenon he had noticed after the battle. He had kept his eyes on the fleeing horses until they had disappeared in the distance. But these pieces of horse-flesh had disappeared long before reaching a size too small to be detected by the human eye. They had blurred and vanished while still distinctly discernible! The performance smacked of something from Omega's bag of tricks. And so it followed that the occurrence was the work of the Russians.

Besides if the horses were flesh-and-blood imitations of the real thing—as Omega would have created—there would be no reason for going to the trouble of causing the disappearance. The Russians would have just left them to run wild. But the fact that they did disappear practically proved his forming theory.

The horses—and the nomads—were not of flesh and blood, but only hypnotic creations forced upon the minds of the Norsemen and himself. And the slain bodies of the nomads persisted because of post-hypnotic suggestion, a thing under-stood even in his day. The horses, no longer needed in the illu-sion, were allowed to vanish as if they had never existed, which indeed they hadn't.

The question then arose as to whether an hypnotic suggestion could do bodily injury. The answer to that came just as readily. It had and therefore it could.

He remembered back before his long sleep that there were hypnotists who could render a subject totally insensible to pain, and who could even pierce the body of the subject with sharp knives and leave no sign of a wound. If this could be done by gifted mortals of his day, it was certainly logical that the terrifically powerful composite brains of the Russians could do the opposite—make wounds by hypnotic suggestion.

The fact that men had been killed and others wounded by powerful hypnotic thoughts infuriated Mark; but it did give him an idea. In the case of another encounter with these solid-seeming phantoms he might now pre-sow seeds that would prevent any more shedding of Viking blood.

"Did you notice how dull their weapons were?" he asked Sven, who was marching at his side.

"Not particularly," Sven admitted. "Were they?"

Mark nodded.

"Yes indeed. Those men were Mongols, and I know them of old. And one thing they never have mastered is the art of sharpening steel weapons. Look at the dent in your helmet. A sharp sword would have cut it in half. And look at the wounds of Olaf and Haldar. They are shallow cuts and yet I distinctly saw the blows struck and they were powerful. Then too, for twenty mounted men to merely dispose of two of our number testifies in itself that their swords would not slice hot lard."

THE ENTIRE band had been listening to Mark's words and several of them examined the superficial wounds of the men mentioned, and marveled that powerful sword-cuts should be so shallow. The slight dent on Sven's helmet—one which had really been caused by a light blow—further convinced them that Mark was right. The whole party brightened up considerably. Each man now felt equal to a thousand nomads, with steel helmets and leather jackets to protect them from the dull *yataghans*.

Mark's seeds were taking better root than he had hoped. His men were now fortified with the thought that they could not be greatly hurt by the Mongols. It would take a lot of suggestion to overcome this previously implanted idea, if it came to another encounter.

Thoughts of the two who had been killed and the other two, grievously wounded, seemed not to bother them at all. If anything, the small number of the casualties strengthened the idea he had suggested. None of them was astute enough to realize that this was directly due to his quickness in placing the band so as to nullify the advantage of the horses.

He had scarcely finished congratulating himself on the success of his idea, when another shout informed him that another danger was in sight.

This time Mark laughed when be saw the sort of adversary the Russians had thrown in his path, just before them was a gradual slope, accompanied by a sharp narrowing of the ravine. At this point the rocky walls of the cut were evidently so hard that the ancient river responsible for the formation had been forced to wear a deeper path for a stretch.

And directly in the middle of this narrow stretch, completely blocking their path, was an enormous dragon! No other name could describe the creature. It had all the formidable appearance of the imaginary figures woven into a Chinese tapestry. It breathed fire and lashed its sinuous, scale-encrusted tail.

The Vikings gazed in awe at the spectacle and then at the laughter-convulsed Mark. Here was a creation so foreign to their experience that they had no standards to judge it by. But their wise and respected leader evidently thought it a matter for hilarious levity, and accordingly they drowned their fears and tried halfheartedly to join in his mirth.

Mark controlled his spasm. This might not be a laughing matter after all. But then he mustn't think such things or the beast would be able to hurt them. He *knew*—knew positively—

that here was but a figment of a controlled imagination, and harmless—so long as he recognized it as such.

For the Russians had overstepped themselves this time. They had proved, by the creation of this outlandish apparition, that they were employing hypnotism and not creating material adversaries for him. Where he had been guessing—and hoping—he now *knew*. And the knowledge further fortified the plan he had for their destruction.

"But what is it?" queried Sven, not quite sure but what his leader might be mistaken about the innocuous character of this beast.

"That is a dragon," explained Mark. "A fabulous, creature that never really existed. This one"—he hesitated, not eager to continue, but seeing no other way out of it—"has been placed in our path to test our courage and steadfastness of purpose. Perhaps Odin; maybe Thor; who knows? Stay here, and I shall slay the creature!"

But the creature refused to wait to be slayed. As Mark confidently strode forward, a tremendous gush of flame emerged from its nostrils!

For a second Mark was hidden from the view of the Vikings and they gasped in dismay. But the flame died away and they saw him, still advancing. What followed left them without even breath enough to gasp. For Mark raised his axe and threw it directly at the eyes of the dragon. And in the instant that the axe should have cleaved the reptilian skull, the apparition vanished!

Mark, beckoning his followers to join him, was elated. When the flame enveloped him, he had felt a tremendous power hammer at his brain, similar to, but weaker than, that he had felt when Omega had forced knowledge of a complete language into his mind. And with this hammer blow had come the physical consciousness that the air was heating about him. The thought seemed to be sledging into his mind that he was to be burnt to a crisp, utterly consumed, in this conflagration.

But to combat this insidious idea was the ever-present knowledge that the whole performance was a fraud; that there was no dragon and the fire really did not exist. And when he had thrown the axe, he had felt another impression—this one much weaker, and very likely unintentional. This new thought conveyed a feeling of frustration.

HE HAD, he realized, won only the first rounds of the battle. Much depended on the amount of knowledge possessed by the Russians. They knew, it was certain, that this party of Norsemen were out for revenge. That was evident—and easily explainable.

The Russians had merely to listen to the conversations of his men to know that. But did they know that he had divined their weakness? And did they know that he had fortified his men against another attack by their Mongols? If they did not, then they might use the nomads again, and he fervently hoped they would. For the Russians could easily circumvent him by conjuring up some sudden, but perfectly plausible disaster. Something which might engulf them before he realized that it was their work.

The Norsemen were frankly adoring since his outstanding feat of monster slaying. And in spite of himself he liked it. For he knew that in a small measure he deserved their admiration. There had been a tiny, gnawing doubt in his mind when those flames had wrapped about him. A doubt that he would emerge unscathed. And it was probably this rebellious thought, however submerged it had been, which had caused him to feel even the slightest heat from that imaginary flame.

The old river bed widened as they went on. The formation could hardly be called a ravine any more. It was a depressed area in an otherwise flat countryside, but they continued to follow its turnings and windings.

It was late in the afternoon when Mark's eye was caught by a reflection of the sun's rays striking a peculiar, domed structure off to the left. Could this be what they were seeking? There was nothing to do but investigate. It certainly wouldn't do to risk passing it. This might be what Omega had meant when he said that he would know when he got there.

Mark ordered the change in direction, peering into the reflection in an effort to see the details of the thing that caused it. At first this was impossible, but as they scrambled up the sloping bank of the dry river bed, the angle of the sun's rays changed, making the reflection less intense.

The formation was unmistakably a manmade structure. Completely dome-shaped, and covering an area somewhat larger than the dome of the old White House at Washington, the thing appeared to be made of some sort of shiny metal. He couldn't be sure, at first, whether this was a building in itself, or if it was merely the domed roof in some enormous structure which had been partially covered by the silt of thousands of years.

It wasn't until they had walked around to the other side of the thing that the question was settled. It was undoubtedly a complete building in itself, for here before them was a door, curved to match the lines of the dome.

Mark didn't realize how large the thing was until he pulled aside the door and stepped in. It was a vast place only dimly lighted by slanting rays which were entering a transparent segment of the roof. But most surprising of all was the fact that the place was completely and starkly empty!

CHAPTER XVII

THE REAL FIGHT

FOR THE FIRST time since his awakening, Mark felt a sensation of weakness. When he had recognized this structure as having been the work of men, he had been certain that here was the end of his quest. And when he had entered the doorway his nerves had been keyed to a fine edge in the expectation of confronting the malignant brains. But here was... nothing.

The Norsemen were evidently experiencing a similar let down. Each had bravely strode through the portal, axe in hand, not knowing what to expect; and they were now gazing aimlessly about the empty interior, their faces mirroring emotions which ranged from acute disappointment to resignation.

Mark was looking disconsolately toward a point directly in the center of the curved floor.

It was here that he had pictured, even before entering, the citadel of the brains. Right at that spot they would have been; enclosed in glass he had thought they would be; two globular crystal containers enclosing human brains, twelve in each, immersed in a greenish fluid. And the whole arrangement, would be mounted on a broad platform, raised from the floor.

Abruptly he realized that he was actually seeing the things he had pictured in his mind. Shimmeringly the vision was taking form!

In a flash his mind sought and found the answer to the amazing phenomenon. No—two answers. The Russians, as a precaution against his band, had assumed a cloak of invisibility. Not actual invisibility, but rather a thought projected into their minds that the place was empty.

He had no guard against that sort of suggestion and it was done without his knowing it. Then, when he looked so fixedly at the spot where they were enshrined, they assumed that he was seeing through the deception and withdrew the hypnotic suggestion as useless. The other solution—and it seemed the more tenable, considering that he had pictured the containers with such uncanny accuracy—indicated that the fine Lunarian hand of Omega might be involved somewhere.

He was considerably heartened by the thought.

But no sooner had the brains become visible than a wall came between him and the sight. A wall of charging Mongols!

With a mad shout that had been heard at Copenhagen and a thousand other places where Norsemen had fought, the

Vikings brandished axes and advanced in a solid body to meet the charge. They needed no orders to fight this sort of battle.

The attackers were not mounted, nor were they seemingly directed by any coherent plan of battle. They merely charged in a straggling rush, mouthing war-cries that daunted the Norsemen not in the least. Though outnumbered five to one, Mark's men advanced steadily in a wedge formation that immediately closed up as the enemy showed signs of clumsily executing a flanking movement.

There was no desperation in their faces. Instead there was the look of unholy joy that they were to be given the opportunity to make mincemeat of the Mongols, and thus gain the revenge for which they thirsted.

And much mincemeat was made.

The Vikings, calm with the knowledge that the armament of the enemy was inferior to their own keen axes and swords, went about their business with deliberate efficiency. Mark found himself at the point of the advancing wedge, slashing vigorously with his flashing axe and glancing at every opportunity toward the platform which was getting nearer and nearer.

It wouldn't be long until he would get a chance to test the hardness of the glass that enclosed the brooding brains of those monsters who had caused so much suffering on this and other worlds.

But there seemed to be arising a new spirit among the Mongols.

They were fighting with a fresh vigor that had almost stopped the steady advance of the Norsemen. And the slashing blows of the *yataghans*, which had been ineffectual up to now—mainly because the Vikings were convinced that the edges were too dull to penetrate—were beginning to draw blood from Mark's men.

He also noticed that the nomads were appearing in ever increasing numbers. Dismayed, he renewed the vigor of his own attack.

HIS RACING mind realized what was happening. The Russians had noted that the Vikings were not falling, mortally wounded, with the cuts of the *yataghans*, and had evidently deduced that they were fortified with the belief that these were not very effective weapons.

So, without changing the type of weapon or the attackers, they had caused the Mongols to appear to be striking much harder blows. Naturally the Vikings would be injured by such blows, for they could see the force with which they were struck and the suggestion in their minds that even the dullest of weapons could thus inflict punishment, would be accepted without question.

If only his mind was sufficiently trained or sufficiently powerful to banish the suggestions of the Russians, he might be able to reach and destroy them before any more damage was done.

But although he refused to allow the Mongol apparitions who struck at him to inflict a single wound, nevertheless he was unable to deny their existence altogether. He could deny their power to hurt him. In fact he sometimes deliberately allowed one to aim a blow at his head, to test his ability to deny the existence of the wielder.

The blow never was so much as felt. But when he tried to walk through one of the apparitions, he found that he must first use physical force to remove the obstacle.

He was getting frantic as he saw his fine hopes go glimmering, and from the knowledge that his comrades were being wounded, perhaps killed, at his back. Progress had now come to a complete stop.

Bodies of Mongols he had killed were at his feet, and every time he would try to get them out of his way, fresh reserves would hammer at him. The hammering was now becoming acutely painful inside his skull, as well. It seemed that one of the composite intellects was devoting all his attention to stopping him personally, while the other carried on the sham battle with the others. His senses were reeling with the repeated blows at his mind.

How could he hope to gain ascendency over this mighty intellect, made up of twelve human brains and with six thousand years of mental exercise to draw from?

More hypnotic suggestion…. He couldn't win…. Better to go back to the ship and leave these others to fight the battle.

The Russians would allow him to live in peace if he would leave them alone. After all these Vikings were no flesh and blood of his. In fact they were pretty dull fellows, when you thought it over. He wouldn't enjoy a lifetime among them at all. Better to desert while there was still time.

Dimly Mark, through sheer habit, continued slashing at the Mongol forms. His arms moved with a volition all their own. Axe slash with the right, and sword cut with the left. The Mongols were pushing their own dead aside to get at him. But he piled them up just the same. They seemed a bit more solid now. He was beginning to feel their blows. Dimly… not hard. Of course not. They couldn't hurt him! He was imagining things. With a sideward twist of his head he glanced back to see how the others were doing.

Good…. Excellent!

There were more Vikings now than there were when he had entered this accursed building. He downed another Mongol, but not before the other had dealt him a resounding blow on the helmet. That hurt, but somehow it cleared his head just a bit. It shouldn't have hurt. He knew that in the instant he had turned to look behind him, he had let down in his fight against the hammering waves that were beating at his brain. In that second he had forgotten that the Mongols were phantoms. And he had forgotten something else. There couldn't be more Vikings than he had brought with him! Omega was here!

GOOD OLD Omega! Creating real Vikings, to fight the spurious Mongols. He risked another glance. His own force was being shouldered out of the way by these newcomers, and being protected by their blades. Good—they needed a rest. They were not tireless like him. But maybe he wasn't as tireless as he thought. There did seem to be a weariness in his arms. He couldn't hit as hard as he had. Maybe this new blood couldn't replace worn-out tissue as quickly as Omega had said.

Might not be such a bad idea to sort of let the replacements surround him and get a little rest. Let the newcomers carry on this fight for a while.

In fact it might be a good idea to have the remains of his original band retire to the ship. Omega could handle these Bolsheviks by himself, now that he knew that they weren't as strong as he had assumed. Of course. And then, back on the ship was Nona. He could see the aching warmth of her glad smile. She was in his arms, her soft flesh pressed against him— and he was kissing her, stroking her hair, her shoulders, his arms clamped around her waist. Her fragrance was like a delicious cloud about him, making him drunk....

Abruptly his brain cleared. These thoughts were not his. And with the knowledge his feeling of lassitude left, and new strength flowed through his body.

They were trying to make him think they would allow him peace if he deserted. But they wouldn't. They evidently thought they could take care of Omega alone, once they could get rid of him. But the suggested thought of Nona's welcome had undone all the progress they had made in his mind.

It brought back the realization that Nona and all the future happiness that Nona stood for was jeopardized.

He slashed out savagely with both weapons. And the fact that he now knew that he had the upper hand caused the Mongols to fall back at his furious attack. Why? Were they not controlled by the Russians? Would the Russians allow them to retreat, even a step? The answer must be that the sore-pressed pair were having their hands full at the moment combating the mind-force of Omega.

In that case Mark could only be seeing these Mongols

because of a posthypnotic suggestion that he must continue to see Mongols barring his progress.

And the Mongols had fallen back because any flesh and blood creature—such as they represented—had to fall back before such a savage assault. Dropping his arms, he faced the platform, a grim smile on his lips. No post-hypnotic suggestion could stop him now. Ignoring the Mongols he moved directly into them.

Hastily, they stepped aside. Mark laughed savagely. *He* was controlling them now! Even if they wouldn't disappear, as they should, they at least had no more power to stop him.

With deliberate step he approached the platform. It was only ten feet away now.

He could see the twin containers with their hellish residents. Dimly visible through the greenish liquid, they looked like fat, horrible sausages with a dozen links each. The greenish fluid took on a tinge of red as his rage at these malignant excrescences grew.

With a savage snarl he drew back his axe, and crashed it into the nearer of the crystal globes. A sudden blow of numbing force struck his brain when the glass shuttered and the fluid gushed forth. It was the last dying effort of a doomed intellect, for the numbness left immediately.

But when he advanced upon the next crystal he was met with a force that was far from feeble.

The shock of its impact blinded him for a moment, so great was its intensity. But only for a moment.

His sight returned and he found himself staring at the remaining container. Its greenish liquid was in a constant motion, swirling endlessly about the linked brains. He wondered which of the Russians this was the biologist or the assistant. It mattered not; he was paralyzed; couldn't move a muscle.

Within the range of his vision was his axe, half raised to strike the final blow.

BUT COULD he move it? No! The arm was as rigid as if made

of steel. He stared into the crystal globe, fighting for consciousness. This was a strain that made the sudden acquisition of a
language seem child's play. But there was one consolation—he
was holding his own. If he couldn't move, neither could the
other blank out his consciousness.

Dimly he realized that the fighting had ceased and the
Vikings were gazing wonderingly at this strange tableau. The
Mongols had probably vanished into the nothingness from
which they had sprung.

But where was Omega?

One would think that as long as he had done as much as he
had, he would do more and blast this lone opponent. Possibly
he knew that success lay within the reach of Mark's hand, and
was standing by to see the outcome. For several moments Mark
found it necessary to abandon this line of thought and concen-
trate all his energy on keeping conscious. This lad certainly
wasn't letting up on him.

He still remained in the rigid posture that the intelligence
had arrested. The arm was still half raised. Suddenly the solution
struck him.

This entity could hold him here forever, for it was tireless
too. And he could stay conscious forever. Even against this
mighty opponent, for his blood was building up brain tissue as
fast as it was being used up in the effort. But his adversary was
dividing his efforts—causing the paralysis, and at the same time
trying to render Mark unconscious. And the brain was having
all it could do to keep both actions maintained.

Mark was kept busy staying awake, without trying to combat
the paralysis.

Suppose something distracted the attention of the entity?
And caused some of the already taxed mental power to be di-
verted? Then obviously, Mark would have some freedom, and
possibly be able to strike the necessary blow. But what might
cause such a distraction? No sooner did the question present
itself than the diversion occurred.

Sven, bleeding from a dozen wounds, decided that if Mark had destroyed one of the crystal globes, then it was the other which was holding him enchanted.

And accordingly the blond giant leaped into action, yowling like a lunatic. But before he had taken three steps, he stopped suddenly, immobile. Mark's pulses gave a jump.

Concentrating mightily, he tried to bring his axe back further to strike a crashing blow. The arm barely moved. He had some freedom, but not enough! Even if he now brought the axe down, it would never shatter the container.

Turgidly the greenish liquid boiled as he strove against its hellish occupant, he was winning! The axe moved faster upward as he brought the arm back.

Two more Vikings had seen his trouble and tried to help. They were both stopped in mid-rush, but the added strain on the composite brain took some of the power it needed to hold Mark.

Then, as three more Norsemen made the effort, Mark suddenly felt free, and in a brief flash shattered the crystal.

A weird, wailing mental vibration gripped him for another instant, but vanished with the death of the cruel intelligence.

CHAPTER XVIII

TOMORROW CAN COME

SIX DAZED NORSEMEN picked themselves off the floor as the paralysis left them. Mark looked jubilantly about to see what form Omega had taken this time. A brawny Swede stepped forth from the ranks of the reinforcements, grinning all over his homely face.

"Howdy, fella," said the newcomer. "Congratulations. I couldn't resist coming to watch the fun."

"Fun!" Mark snorted but his eyes conveyed his gratitude.

"Nice of you to show up. They about had me licked till you came along."

"Nonsense! You didn't need me at all. I didn't pit my mind against theirs for an instant. You did it all yourself. But tell me how you figured you could lick them. I still don't see it. By what line of reasoning were you so sure they would die, instead of living as pure thought patterns?"

Mark looked at him quizzically, wearily gave orders for the march back to the ship, and then tried to explain.

"The idea never occurred to you until I suggested it. And yet if your brain had been destroyed in your absence would you have died when you found it out? No. You would have realized instantly that you had been living without it and would therefore continue to. But if you had been attacked, by some material enemy while residing within it, and that enemy had smashed your brain you would have died without ever considering that the thing might not be essential to your existence.

"Working on these lines I realized that it was necessary to destroy the Russians while they were at home, so to speak. That was why I took the gang along. They would be sure to spot us and arrange a welcome. I had been giving the thing some thought on the trans-Atlantic trip, but the idea never came to me, full-blown, until we landed and I saw the suffering those monsters had caused. And realized that my own descendants would receive no better treatment."

Omega, trudging along beside Mark, shook his head in amazed admiration.

"You've a much longer alimentary canal than I ever had," he remarked.

"I don't know just how that is to be interpreted, but if you mean 'more guts,' I won't be offended."

"It's not so bad in Swedish. But how were you so sure they wouldn't utterly destroy you along the way? An avalanche or some such thing."

"Well I had to take a chance on that. But you will remember

that the Russians had been having their own way for many a year, and wouldn't be likely to think that ordinary humans could harm them. For that reason and also because I already knew that they loved to exercise their seemingly endless powers to cause human suffering. I figured that they would decide to play with us for a while before destroying us. Of course, it was a long chance, but it worked out all right."

Omega chuckled. "It seems it did. I wouldn't have missed it for anything. It proves my assertion that any race with such a strong will to live and such unselfish courage in its individuals, is worth giving a boost to. And I'm glad I let you fight the battle yourself. You didn't need me, anyway."

Mark grinned. "Hope you're around the next time that I don't need you," he said.

"I will be," Omega assured him, with a sly twinkle in his eye. "At the christening!"

The party was forced to camp with the approach of night. Mark looked at the sleeping reinforcements with satisfaction. They had existed for only a few hours but Omega had fitted them with brains equal to those of their natural born companions. They would be accepted into the community and no doubt some of the women would eventually forget their grief to mate with them. The dead could not be replaced, but these newcomers would help fill in the gap.

His thoughts turned to Nona, who was waiting anxiously for his return. Life would be something worth living now. He had earned the right to live it.

LET 'EM EAT SPACE

Just a few plush-lined seats left on the space ship—and well worth scrambling for. Today's excursion takes us to Propus, where shadows eat rabbits and you meet the nicest, wackiest people found on any planet.

MR. MONTGOMERY, FIRST vice-president of Interplanetary Insurance, Incorporated, was gazing in a severe and somewhat disapproving manner over the upper rim of his horn-rimmed spectacles. Across the polished desk fidgeted Mr. Ham Eggles, small and dapper, and Mr. Slim Winters, tall, thin and unkempt.

Ham, with a small portion of his mind, was wondering what would happen if Mr. Montgomery ever should happen to look through those specs. By far the greater part of his gray matter, however, was engaged in pleasant contemplation of the charms of a certain barmaid of his acquaintance.

Slim, on the other hand, was a man who invariably concentrated on the matter at hand. He was busy worrying why the boss had summoned them.

Mr. Montgomery cleared his throat. "I suppose," he said, "that you gentlemen are familiar with the phenomenon of metabolism."

Ham looked at Slim and Slim looked at Ham. "Why sure," they chorused; then abruptly fell into an embarrassed silence.

"Yes, of course," said Mr. Montgomery dryly. "I knew also, after I had consulted a dictionary. But I'll save you that trouble. Metabolism is the process of building up and breaking down of tissues and cells in living organisms. It constitutes the vital chemical processes of life itself."

His audience revealed by facial expression that it had heard of some such thing back in its school days.

"Now that you thoroughly understand the subject," continued the boss, "you will probably be interested to know that it has slowed up."

"What has?" queried Ham, absently.

"Metabolism, you rum-soaked Casanova!" supplied Slim.

"This fact came to us as a result of diligent investigation on the part of our research department," said Mr. Montgomery, ignoring the by-play.

"We have been deluged with industrial claims that have been pouring in from all over the solar system. This unexpected departure from normal began in the spring of 2074, over a year ago. We have traced the cause of most of the accidents to a lack of alertness and agility on the part of the victims. Workers are no longer able to keep up with their machines.

"All sorts of things have been happening. Men are getting their hands taken off in punch presses; airplanes are making poor landings; bus drivers are getting in accidents, trying to make their schedules. In short, wherever men are engaged in work with machines which are normally geared to keep pace with human ability, they are having trouble."

Mr. Montgomery leveled an accusing finger.

"It has also come to light that men engaged in sound research, in connection with the cinema and radio industries, have found that women who formerly sang soprano are now baritones, and men who were baritones are now making sounds far below the audible range of normal hearing. And yet the ear has failed to detect any change.

"WITH THESE facts to work on, we soon discovered that the reason for the condition lies in the fact that metabolism has slowed up. Further investigation has proven that all life in the solar system has been similarly affected. To sum up the situation: life has been slowed down to a crawl. And we must do something about it!"

Ham, down again, let out a yelp; but Slim made
the jump in time and turned to lend a hand.

He emphasized his words with a resounding thump on the
desk with a balled fist. Slim and Ham were looking slightly
bewildered by this time, for metabolism, a purely biological
business, was entirely out of their scope. Slim hesitantly advanced this information.

"I'm coming to that," said the boss. "As I mentioned, we must
do something about this deplorable situation. For although the
company has weathered the storm of claims, and keeping in
mind that mankind is becoming accustomed to the slower rate
of metabolism, we have no assurance that the thing may not
occur again. We could scarcely hope to retain our solvency if
that happened.

"And then, too," he added, as an afterthought of little consequence, "mankind might not survive another such drastic
change.

"But to continue: our research workers have further discovered that concurrent with the deluge of accident claims, certain

scientists reported a sharp decrease in the amount of cosmic rays which reach the solar system. The inference is obvious—that the rate of metabolism is directly dependent upon intensity of cosmic rays absorbed by the living being.

"And there," the boss concluded, "is where you gentlemen enter the picture. It is your job to determine the cause of the decreased density of these rays."

Ham remained in a state of bewilderment—at least that portion of his mind which was not lingering on the aforementioned barmaid. The problem of the cosmic rays seemed as remote from his field as had the matter of metabolism. For he and Slim were not engaged by the company as scientists or research workers, but rather as detectives, confining their activities to doubtful claims in various parts of the solar system.

But where Ham failed to see the connection, Slim apparently grasped the idea immediately.

"You mean… interstellar space?"

"Precisely. Cosmic rays originate far outside the solar system, and you'll have to follow them if you intend to learn anything. Our experts will give you all the necessary information.

"Your ship is equipped with the most modern of gravity drives, capable of many times the speed of light. The latest space-warp principle will be incorporated into the design of the drive. That will take only a few days. You are to use it, of course, only after you are well out of the system."

CHAPTER II

SOMEWHAT LESS THAN a week later, a silvery torpedo may have been seen flashing past the outermost planet of the solar system.

But if it was seen at all, it couldn't have been observed for any great length of time. For shortly after passing the orbit of the most distant rampart of old Sol, the ship surpassed the speed of light itself, immediately becoming invisible to any observer in the rear of its line of flight.

Ham was staring contentedly ahead into the void, through which they were rushing with such speed that the light of the stars ahead was of a decided bluish tinge, when a frown came to mar his usual serenity of countenance.

"I know it's none of my business," he complained to Slim, "but if it's not too much to ask, just where the heck are we headed for?"

The elongated one lifted his eyes momentarily from a sheaf of astronomical charts and grunted, "Eta Geminorum, Propus!"

"Never heard of it," remarked Ham, returning to his stargazing.

"A Cepheid variable of the long-period variety," informed Slim. "Has a period of 231.4 days during which it varies in magnitude from 3.2 to 4.2."

Ham continued staring for several minutes before his placidly preoccupied mind digested this. Slim was always babbling miscellaneous bits of information, interesting to him at the moment; and Ham had developed the faculty of completely ignoring him, especially when he had something on his own mind.

But when the intelligence did finally sink in, he snapped to attention.

"That's quite a ways out, isn't it?" he asked. "Is that where the cosmic ray experts said we'd find the trouble?"

Slim slowly uncoiled himself, deserting the charts, and rose to creakily stretch his great length. He was about six feet six, and so thin that Ham always insisted that he had to stand still for at least five minutes to cast a visible shadow.

"That's what they said, little one," affirmed Slim. "I should think you'd take more interest in these minor details. You've been acting as if this little jaunt were in the nature of a pleasure trip."

"It probably is. I don't see what we can do about it, anyway.

We didn't even know we had slowed up until old specs-on-the-nose told us. And neither does anybody else. By the time we get back people will be completely adjusted to the slower rate of metabolism. Or the machines will be adjusted, which amounts to the same thing. I can't see where the matter is of any great importance."

"You can't, eh? Suppose the thing happens again? Suppose the rays decrease until metabolism is slowed down to about one-third. Humanity would be very likely to suffer a fatal attack of indigestion."

Patiently, Slim explained.

"In the normal operation of the human body, a series of complicated chemical processes are constantly in progress. And the whole works would be thrown out of kilter by such a drastic departure from the proper speed of anabolism and katabolism."

"You certainly know a lot of words," Ham commented, not greatly concerned by the dire prospect. "But what has all that to do with this variable star we're heading for?"

Slim chuckled. Ham's question took a lot more words to answer.

"LOOK," HE said, "It's believed that the cause of the decreased cosmic ray intensity lies somewhere in the vicinity of that star. Science has long been aware that the rays are sent out by every one of the Cepheid variables. Just why, is not known. But the inference is that whatever force causes these peculiar stars to pulsate, also generates the rays in enormous quantities.

"It has been observed that the short-period Cepheids appear to emit the greater number of rays. Of these, Zeta Geminorum is about the most active. On the other hand, the long-period variables gives off very few of the rays. All but one, and that's the one we're going to investigate.

"Propus, unbelievably, has always furnished the solar system with as great an intensity of cosmic rays as all of the other variables put together. And now, practically overnight, Propus diminishes its output to a point comparable with other long-period variables of similar size."

"Unbelievable!" mocked Ham.

"Don't be so darned flippant," exclaimed Slim, somewhat exasperated. "The fate of humanity is at stake if the thing should go any further."

"Not according to what you told me," said Ham. "The solar system is receiving its present diminished supply from the other Cepheids, and is managing to get along just the same. The mysterious decrease from Propus isn't likely to be repeated over such a widely scattered area. My deduction is that the tremendous output from that star was an unstable phenomenon, and something happened to restore it to normal. Logical, what?"

Slim clasped and unclasped his hands several times, meanwhile looking very thoughtful. He then grunted eloquently and sat down to resume study of the star charts.

"While you're looking at those road maps," Ham suggested, "see if you can find if our shrinking violet has any planets, and if so, how big."

Slim grunted again, riffled the charts and picked out the desired one. "The best telescope ever developed couldn't see a planet small enough for us to stand up on, at that distance. The chart shows one planet, about the size of Jupiter, and notes that there are probably four more. Maybe one of them will be our size."

The chart-maker turned out to be a fairly accurate guesser. The travelers were able to spot four satellites of the pulsating luminary, including the one shown on the map. It was altogether possible that there was one or two more, either extremely distant from their sun, or of very low albedo.

But they weren't greatly interested in the possibility, for their attention was immediately attracted to the second world in the system.

Approximately nine thousand miles in diameter it gave off a bluish-green light, similar to that of the earth, when seen from a proximity of a few million miles. The resemblance decided them. They would land.

If intelligent life was to be found in the system, this seemed the most likely place to find it. Slim was on fire with the thought that he might be able to communicate with the denizens of this planet, and learn from them the reason for their sun's peculiar actions.

AS THE ship approached, the planet's resemblance to earth became even more marked. There were mighty oceans, vast forests and even greater areas of arid desert. The proportion of water to land was somewhat less, indicating greater age; but it was still a fair substitute for Mother Earth.

"There's one thing missing," Slim noticed.

"Cities," supplied Ham. "I've been looking for them."

"Wait'll we get closer. Maybe they don't live in cities."

"Maybe they don't. And then again, maybe there aren't any 'they'."

But there were. As the ship neared the planet it became evident that some sort of a civilization was flourishing below them. Scattered widely over the surface of this world, were hundreds of large buildings of peculiar construction.

There seemed to be no system to their distribution, for they were situated in the most unusual spots. Invariably dome-shaped, and of a grayish-white color, the structures were just as likely to be seen in the middle of a desert, or perched precariously on the side of a mountain, as in a more conventional position.

"Look at that one!" Slim pointed. "Tilted on its edge, and half buried in the side of that hill!"

"Looks like the inhabitants of this sphere are among the dear departed," Ham guessed. "It's a cinch they didn't build those things in such dizzy places. More likely they've been there for thousands of years, and the topography of the land has altered."

"I guess so," admitted Slim, gloomily. "They weren't built for human use anyway. I haven't seen a window or door in any of them."

"Well, let's land, get into one of them, and take some pictures."

It was several minutes before they decided on one of the structures, situated in a desirable spot. The one selected lay almost in the center of a broad, grassy plain, and they picked it because a clear view was to be had for miles in all directions. If there happened to be any dangerous animal life on the planet they wouldn't be caught unaware.

The ship landed about a hundred yards from the curious structure.

Slim turned off the gravity controls, and they took a few cautious steps.

"Don't notice any difference," Ham remarked. "Should be heavier."

"Maybe this planet is composed of lighter materials," Slim hazarded, busy with the analysis of a sample of the outside air. "You can't always depend on size. Look at that little baby that balances Sirius. Smaller than the earth, and heavier than the sun."

"You look at it. How's the air?" piped Ham.

"Nineteen percent oxygen, and three percent carbon dioxide. The rest is helium, except for small quantities of some of the rarer gases found in our own atmosphere. Pressure, about seventeen pounds."

"Ought to be breathable," decided Ham. "Bring the torch."

He released the latches on the inner airlock door, while Slim produced the torch from a locker. The outer door followed, and in a minute they had jumped to the ground and were breathing the air of the new planet.

They wasted no time looking around them, but set out immediately to cover the short distance to the hive-like building. Slim was carrying the torch, with which they intended to burn their way inside; Ham was lugging a camera and a few dozen flash bulbs. They were about half-way to the structure when involuntarily both stopped dead in their tracks.

CHAPTER III

"I THOUGHT THAT was a rock!" exclaimed Ham, gazing in consternation at an object slightly to the right of their path. The object, about three feet in diameter and smoothly rounded, when they first sighted it, was now about five feet long and as thick through as Ham's thigh.

"Looks more like a worm to me," said Slim, judiciously, "Except that it's brown—although that could be sun-tan."

"Which end is which?" inquired Ham.

"Neither. A worm's the same on each end. You have to wait until it moves, and even then you might be fooled. It might be backing up."

But it became immediately apparent that this system, admittedly unreliable, was less than useless in the case at hand. For the worm moved, and in a quite unpredictable manner. Its opposite sides bulged and kept bulging until it resembled a four-pointed starfish.

"It'll never get anywhere that way," was Ham's comment.

"Maybe it's not going anywhere. Maybe it wants to hear you make some more silly remarks. Come on."

"But suppose this is an intelligent creature?" suggested Ham "Maybe we should try to communicate with it."

"Phooey! That's an amoeba-like animal on the order of those creatures that infest the marshes of Venus, except for the healthy color and the larger size. They live sluggishly by ingesting nourishment from the grasses and other vegetation with which their bodies come in contact. Reproduce by fission."

"You seem well acquainted around here," Ham murmured.

But inasmuch as the strange creature seemed satisfied to retain his star-fish shape, and made no further effort to be entertaining, Ham decided that Slim was probably right, and the two resumed their former course.

They had taken only a few steps, when they were again brought up short. They both distinctly heard the word, "Wait!" They looked at each other, each thinking for a brief instant that the other had spoken. Then the answer dawned on them.

"It was the worm!" Slim exclaimed.

"You mean the ameba-like creature," corrected Ham, sarcastically.

"Which is correct," informed the starfish. "My composition is very similar to the picture your mind gives me of the amoeba."

The two voyagers looked incredulously at the astounding creature. Their astonishment was due to the fact that they now realized the thing was causing the words to be formed in their minds, and making no audible sound while doing it.

Such an accomplishment had often been imagined, and indeed it was believed that certain men had abilities in that direction; but neither had ever encountered the phenomenon and the experience was eerie in the extreme.

"Did I hear you infer that you can read our minds?" Slim finally queried.

"**NOT YOUR** ordinary thoughts," explained the ameba. "They are not strong enough to transmit themselves. But I do receive impressions when you speak, for the effort expended makes the waves stronger. And of course I can make my own thoughts strong enough to impress them on your primitive minds."

Slim turned to Ham. "I think he's pulling our collective leg. What could be more primitive than an ameba?"

"But there's nothing primitive about telepathy," Ham reminded.

"And I didn't say that I was an amoeba," corrected the creature. "I merely said that I am similar to one. As a matter of fact, my people represent the evolution of that unicellular form carried out to the nth degree."

"Then you, personally, are not unicellular?" deduced Ham.

"No more than you are."

The starfish stretched forth one of its members for their examination. "You will notice that my skin is of a rubbery nature, and quite tangible and opaque. The unicellular creature is transparent, and the outer covering is so tenuous that it readily allows food and moisture to pass through.

"The amoeba, as such, is strictly limited as far as size is concerned. Its cell walls would break down from its own weight if it grew too much. So obviously I am constructed of many cells."

"Sounds reasonable," Slim admitted. "But if your skin is so tough, how do you eat? Or don't you need nourishment?"

Again one of the pseudopodia was thrust out, this time bottom side up. There were dozens of small openings on the under side of the member, some of them gaping and closing rhythmically.

The men shuddered involuntarily, for the whole thing looked very much like one of the arms of an octopus. Then, abruptly, all of the openings closed and the rubbery texture of the skin became smooth and unbroken.

"I was only demonstrating," explained the evolved amoeba, apologetically. "The mouths are not there when I don't need them to admit food. Merely a multi-celled adaptation of the unicellular form. Even my brain is but the highly evolved replica of the nucleus of a primitive amoeba."

"If it's not too much to ask," ventured Ham, "do you have, concealed somewhere about your person, a pair of eyes?"

"Nothing so complicated. Instead I see with every nerve on the surface of my body. It is by far the most simple and efficient visional apparatus, for I can see in all directions. All the nerve-ends are sensitive to light."

"Amazing," claimed Ham. "But how about...."

"Wait a minute," Slim broke in. "We're forgetting what we came here for. Maybe this gent knows the answer."

But before either man could put the question to the amoeba,

a feeling of acute alarm swept into their consciousness with such intensity that both cringed as if threatened with instant extinction. They knew that the sensation was caused by a similar feeling in their new acquaintance, but it was none the less real.

"**RUN!.... RUN!**" shrilled the next mental message. And run they did. There was no time wasted in looking about for danger.

Too many times in the course of their interplanetary wanderings they had been in spots where instant flight was the only means of survival; they did not hesitate now.

But before they had covered half the distance to the space ship, an unseen blow from behind knocked them flat. Scrambling wildly to their feet, they fairly flew the rest of the way.

As they were about to leap for the edge of the airlock, Ham let out a yelp as he was again knocked down, this time more forcibly than before. But Slim made the jump, lithely pulled his lanky body up, and turned in time to lend the other a hand.

Slamming the outer door, after hurriedly noting that the amoeba was nowhere to be seen, they stood panting and trembling. Finally Ham, having caught his breath, chuckled at the ludicrous expression of fright on Slim's face.

"Funny, eh?" Slim panted. "I suppose you know what it's all about. What knocked us down, and what became of our pal.... Come on, let me in on it."

Ham sobered and looked out of the nearest port. An empty plain stretched in all directions. Empty, that is, except for the mysterious building and the camera, flash bulbs and torch, which they had dropped when ordered to run. There was no sign of their recent acquaintance, the high evolved amoeba.

"I've sort of run out of ideas," he admitted, shakily.

It was a full hour later, and almost a full quart of Scotch whisky later, when Slim again voiced wonderment at the creature's strange absence from the landscape.

"I wonder what became of Jasper," said he.

Ham dwelt sadly on this mystery as he poured out the last

of the Scotch. For several minutes the silence was broken only by the occasional liquid gurgle of a trickle of Haig and Haig passing an unsteady epiglottis.

Both men were mourning the disappearance, but for different reasons. Slim's mind was wholly filled with the lost opportunity for gaining some knowledge of the strange behavior of Propus; his friend had conceived a genuine—if slightly alcoholic—affection for the missing amoeba.

"He seemed such a friendly sort of a critter," said Ham, half tearfully. "No harm in 'im a-tall."

"And so darned willing to oblige," supplemented Slim. "He was willing to tell all—if we had only been given time to ask him."

"And not only that," enlarged Ham, striding uncertainly toward one of the ports, "but he wasn't impolitely asking us a bunch of questions about our origin. And he must have been very curious about it, too.... Say!"

He broke off, attracted by something outside. "Come here, quick!"

Slim bounded to his feet, almost folded up, but managed to reach the bullet-like window. He arrived just in time to see a small rabbit, or something that looked like a rabbit, come to an untimely end. The animal had been chased, and overtaken, by a shadow.

At least it had seemed to be a shadow while it was in motion, but now as it stopped and engulfed the rabbit in its indefinable blackness, it looked more like a hole in the ground. It was impossible to focus the eyes on the thing.

SLIM BLINKED several times, thinking of the pernicious effects of alcohol on the optic nerve, but was still unable to determine anything about the blob of darkness other than the fact that it appeared to be about the size of the vanished creature he had called Jasper.

"I'll bet that's the jigger that bowled us over," he finally said, turning to Ham, who was futilely trying to coax a few more drops from the bottle.

"Wouldn't be surprised," sighed Ham, returning to the port for another look. "What do you think we should.…. Hey! It has went! What became of it?"

Slim again looked out, but saw nothing of the shadow and no sign of the unfortunate rabbit, if that's what it was.

He explained patiently that he had no part in the phenomenon and that the shadow had certainly been there when he looked away, and followed this intelligence with the suggestion that inasmuch as Propus was getting ready to set, it might be a good idea if they both sought relief from the harrowing memories of the day's happenings, by catching a little sleep.

Ham, with a solemn gravity reminiscent of the bottle, agreed wholeheartedly. Tomorrow, he averred, was another day.

Tomorrow, indeed, was another day; although as events progressed, it turned out to be quite as harrowing as the one it followed.

It was a good twelve hours after the setting of Propus that the first ruddy rays of the morning entered a port and moved to the point where they shone directly on Ham's face. He opened slitted eyes, sat erect and groaned.

But there was no time for him to collect his sense and realize to the fullest how terrible he felt, for a diversion occurred immediately. The light which had awakened him was shut off abruptly; and, quite startled, he got up to investigate.

The port in question was a good ten feet above the ground, and the ship was still situated in the middle of a treeless plain. That he was startled is easy to understand.

For nothing—except a cloud, which would have made the light dim gradually—should have been there to cast that shadow. Uneasy thoughts of the rabbit-killing menace of the night before coursed through his head as he peered through the little window.

"Good morning," greeted a familiar voice.

"It's Jasper!" he muttered, incredulously. And then he saw the obstruction. It was, indeed, Jasper. And that personage was hovering, quite nonchalantly—as if such doings were a regular thing with him, which, of course, was altogether possible—a short distance above the window.

"I don't wish to disturb you," came the emanation. "But will you please let me come inside?"

Ham thought he detected a note of urgency in the message. He seemed to be experiencing, in a slighter degree, the same feeling of horror and fear that had preceded the attack of the day before. He made record time of opening the airlock, admitting the amoeba, who floated eerily past him, and shutting it again.

"I was afraid you wouldn't awake in time," said Jasper, gently settling to the floor. "I was about to be attacked by one of the Mad Ones."

"Why didn't you wake us? Your thoughts seemed to penetrate the walls of the ship easily enough."

"Oh, I wouldn't have considered it! We Jaspers are very considerate of each other's privacy."

CHAPTER IV

HAM'S SLIGHTLY BLOOD-SHOT eyes widened perceptibly. Slim had referred to the amoeba by that name Jasper, not knowing his real one, and now the critter had evidently accepted it for his own.

No... that wasn't it. The amoeba hadn't used a name at all. He was using thoughts. And Ham's mind was automatically translating the thoughts into words, without even realizing it. And the word his mind had given him for the highly evolved amoeba, and all of its kind, was naturally the same one he had mentally been using to designate him.

Further deductive reasoning along those lines was abruptly interrupted by a minor explosion from the direction of Slim's bed. That gentleman had begun to squirm and thrash about as the sound of the conversation penetrated his dim consciousness.

Suddenly he yelled in a fear-filled voice, "Get him off a me!" and sat up, looking a bit sheepish.

"Musta been something I et," he explained, looking with pleased surprise at Jasper. "What became of you last night?"

"I rose in the air, out of harm's way. My people utilize the principle of levitation as a normal function of our bodies."

"Amazing!"

"If you'll remember," suggested Ham, "this is your week to get the meals. Suppose you break out the tomato juice while I converse with our guest. By the way Jasper, is there anything my friend can prepare for you? I don't know whether our sort of food would agree with you."

"Nothing, thank you. I have eaten my usual meal of grasses and require no more."

"Well—in that case let's get back to where we left off. You were about to be attacked by one of the Mad Ones. And what might they be?"

"They are really Jaspers like myself," informed the guest. "Except that they are changed in a horrible and irreversible way. I'll tell you about it. A few hundred years ago, there was a very adventuresome Jasper who wanted to explore into the outer gaseous envelope of our luminary. He protected himself with very strong walls of force surrounding his body, and set out to do this very thing.

"For ordinary travel in space he had taken more than sufficient precautions, for the force-screen he set up about himself was several times the intensity of the ones we Jaspers have been using for millions of years.

"But never before had we undertaken to approach a sun closely, let alone actually enter one. And evidently there was something lacking in his screen, admitting an unknown vibration; for a peculiar mutation occurred in both brain and body."

Jasper's thoughts appeared troubled for a moment, before his discourse continued.

"THIS WASN'T noticed for some time after his return. But when he divided—we follow the same lines of development as the unicellular creature in regards to division by fission—the effects became at once apparent. The two smaller beings became almost invisible, reflecting only the infrared vibrations, and absorbing all the higher ones.

"They also became carnivorous. An unheard-of thing, for we Jaspers respect the right of all living creatures to exist without interference. And to make this change even more horrible, the Mad Ones took to devouring their own brothers, when they were unable to find other animal food.

"They are becoming quite a problem, for since the mutation occurred they have multiplied at a much faster rate than normal Jaspers, and now number almost one-tenth of our population. And all of our ingenuity has failed to find a means of returning the Mad Ones to normal."

Slim looked thoughtfully over the rim of his glass of tomato juice.

"You mentioned 'brothers,'" he observed. "I can easily see how beings who reproduce as you do, would all be brothers— or perhaps fathers or uncles. Is that why it has never occurred to you to exterminate these Mad Ones?"

Jasper didn't answer immediately. Although he possessed no features with which to express emotion, it was evident that Slim's words had shocked him, and probably started a train of thought in an unexplored direction.

"I can see that such a course would be natural to a race of beings who developed under a more competitive environment," he finally said. "But you must understand that such a thing would be abhorrent to my people. We have never known strife; not even mild competition. We have never been faced with the need for fighting with any of the myriad forms of life with which we have come in contact.

"Whenever a Jasper is attacked by a carnivorous life-form, he merely rises and moves to a place where he is safe. So naturally the instinct to kill when menaced has never been developed in us."

"You wouldn't even fight when you know that eventually these Mad Ones will multiply to the point where the planet will be uninhabitable for you?"

"I'm afraid not. I know that I could not kill a Mad One, even if he were eating me. And therefore no other Jasper could, for we are all alike."

"That certainly is a sad state of affairs," Slim commiserated.

"And it looks as if nothing we could think of would be of any help. We're too barbaric."

"Without any intention of offending, I'm afraid you are. And it is not likely that you could help solve the problem in the only way acceptable to us—that of correcting the mutation. For our civilization is millions of years older than yours, and we have spent that time profitably, not in war and strife. And so our minds are much better equipped to reason logically."

"Yet we have failed. Therefore, let us drop the subject and return to the point where we were interrupted yesterday."

The two men looked blankly at each other.

"You were going to tell me what you came here for," supplied Jasper. "You said, 'Maybe this gent knows the answer.'"

Slim grinned broadly and then proceeded to expound volubly on the solar system's metabolism trouble.

"We Jaspers were afraid of that," said the amoeba.

"Then you know what caused the phenomenon. Tell us."

"WE CAUSED it," admitted Jasper. "In fact we caused your race to come into existence, though of course we didn't plan it that way. I'll explain.

"Millions of years past, when the pulsations of our luminary were of much shorter duration, my race came into conscious existence. The property of levitation was ours even then, and to that gift is given credit for our rapid advancement in becoming sentient beings.

"For as we became larger and multicelled, we could avoid the terrible heat of our sun, during its intense periods, by flying through the air and continually keeping on the night side of the planet.

"This enabled the race to continue its mental development, while lesser creatures were forced to go into periods of hiberna-

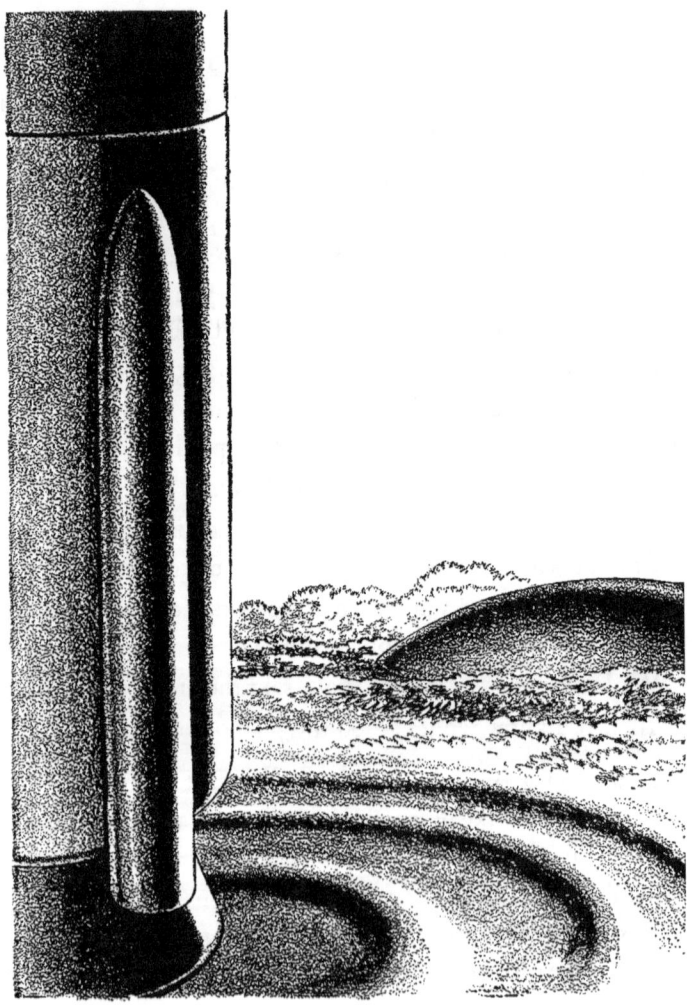

tion when the sun was hot, and spend all of their time stuffing themselves with food when the sun was cool. Our periods of flying became periods of study and mental communion, during which great advancement took place."

"Pardon me a moment," Slim interrupted. "You mean that you flew for days at a time, keeping pace with the planet's rotation? Wouldn't that require a terrific amount of energy?"

"Quite the contrary. Our levitation mechanism operates on the same principle as the gravity drive of your ship. And it takes almost no energy to maintain a warp in the gravitational lines of force of a planet. The chief difference lies in the fact that the mechanism is a normal bodily function with us.

"But to continue. As time went on, and our population increased, it became apparent that new worlds would have to be found. At that time our numbers were doubling—by division, of course—every hundred years, and it was estimated that before another ten thousand years had passed, this planet would become uncomfortably crowded.

"And it was decided that we would choose, for the overflow,

a world in some solar system where it would not be necessary continually to dodge the waxing periods of a pulsating sun.

"Such a world we thought we had found in your own planet. But we knew that your sun gave off but few of the emanations that made life possible to us. I refer to the cosmic rays. Accordingly we set up a tremendous projector at our south pole, which always faces toward your system, to compensate for the deficiency.

"It was necessary to make this projector powerful enough to manufacture many times the quantity of rays that any one Cepheid emits. This, of course, to compensate for the greater distance.

"We were still faced with the problem of taking care of our immediate increase, for it would be many times ten thousand years before your planet would be suitable for us.

"But, tragically, nature solved the problem for us. There came an extended period of volcanic activity on this planet which resulted in the deaths of thousands and thousands of Jaspers. Our population fell off considerably, rather than increasing. But eventually normal circumstances returned and once again we multiplied.

"After a few million years it was decided that your planet should have by then developed the proper sort of plant life to support our race, and accordingly an expedition was sent out to investigate.

"But something had gone wrong. The earth was found to be inhabited by many forms of giant reptilian life, some of them carnivorous. The whole project was therefore a failure. The world was obviously unsuited to us. It was then necessary—"

"**WHOA THERE!**" Slim again interrupted. "You said the expedition found gigantic reptiles. The age of saurians was way back in the Triassic and Jurassic periods, almost two hundred million years ago."

"Oh yes. The projector was built long before that—somewhere in the Carboniferous era!"

"Well why didn't you shut the thing off, once you saw that the earth was covered with the reptiles?" Ham wanted to know.

"But we couldn't do that!" exclaimed the amoeba, sounding a bit horrified. "The reptiles required the rays, and to cease sending them would have been murder."

"And we invent such words as 'altruism,'" was Ham's mumbled comment.

"But the projector was no drain on our resources or our time," Jasper said deprecatingly. "It required no effort to maintain, for it operated by transforming useless emanations of our sun into the desired ones."

"But what finally caused it to cease functioning?" inquired Slim.

"The Mad Ones turned it off. Why, I can't say, for in the vicinity of the machine there is an abundance of game, which they value. But they are quite irrational, and it is useless to conjecture on their motives. Several of my people have made attempts to start the mechanism, fearing that its failure might be causing suffering on your system; but each time they were driven away by the voracious Mad Ones."

Slim looked at Ham and screwed his face into a ludicrous expression of thoughtfulness. After several minutes of this, he evidently came to a momentous decision.

"It looks as if we had better take a trip to the south pole," he announced. "And the sooner, the quicker."

Ham, who had also been giving the matter some thought, saw a few objections.

"And if the place is crawling with Jasper's demented relatives, what do you propose to do? I've always been superstitious about being eaten. Don't think I'd like it—nohow!"

"Contrariwise!" supplemented Slim. "I don't intend to be eaten. I've got an idea."

"Most anything can happen now. All right, you start the ship, and our pal will show the way. Won't you, Jasper?"

"Of course," agreed the amoeba. "But I don't see how...."

"NATURALLY NOT. Beings with your finer instincts couldn't possibly think the things I'm thinking. But let's see if my idea isn't okay. You said that the Mad Ones reflect only infra-red from the surface of their bodies. And absorb all the visual light vibrations.

"My deduction is therefore, that such beings would not be able to stand much light. It would burn them up, inasmuch as light which is absorbed becomes heat. Am I right so far?"

"Yes, I believe you are. The Mad Ones are almost entirely nocturnal creatures. They never come out in the full light of day, and only occasionally in the late afternoon, when the rays of Propus are red and weak."

He hesitated. "But if you are contemplating the use of light rays to kill them, I think I would rather not have anything to do with such an undertaking."

"But I assure you, my dear Jasper, I am by nature as gentle as a lamb. Which reminds me—I was bitten by a lamb once. But he, of course, was a very vicious lamb.

"Here is the situation: We, as humans, wish to start up the cosmic ray apparatus. And that is just what we intend to do. Now, if in the act of so doing we are attacked by anybody at all, we must defend ourselves. Self-preservation is the first law of nature.

"To you, that takes the form of flight. But inasmuch as we are not endowed with the gift of levitation, we would have to fight to defend ourselves. And, knowing what we might have to fight, we would naturally prepare ourselves accordingly.

"Now that doesn't sound like premeditated murder, does it? We certainly are not asking them to attack us. In fact, we will go out of our way to avoid them."

There was a long minute of silence while Jasper weighed the finer moral aspects of the situation. He finally came to a decision, but it was not so much Slim's words as his own sense of responsibility which was the balancing factor.

On Slim's line of reasoning alone, he would still have refrained from having any hand in an act which might result in violence. But there was the annoying thought that the beings of the solar system were suffering because of a condition which was the direct responsibility of his race. And, in all justice, he must make sacrifices to help them.

Even if it meant going counter to his own moral convictions.

In a few minutes the ship was silently winging its way southward. Slim was at the controls, with Jasper hovering at his shoulder, while Ham was busily hooking small atomic generators to a pair of powerful searchlights. When he was finished, he tried them out, producing a light to rival the sun in brilliance, but still he seemed a bit dissatisfied.

He stood surveying his handiwork for a minute, decided the lights were too heavy for easy carrying, and set about to correct the fault by attaching leather straps.

Suddenly he stopped work, partially paralyzed by an idea. "Say!" he erupted. "What are we bothering with these lights for? Why not do our dirty work in the full light of day, about noon, when the Mad Ones are under cover?"

"Because there isn't any full light of day," Slim informed. "The place we are headed for is the south pole, and as you should have noticed, this planet rotates on an axis perpendicular to the plane of the ecliptic.

"Which means, of course, that the south pole region has a night and day of the same duration as at the equator, but receives very little light, even at high noon. Therefore, the Mad Ones are able to travel around without any discomfort all day long."

Ham went back to work, muttering to himself. There was one more thing he wanted to know, but he would be darned if he'd say anything and give Slim a chance to pop out the answer in his superior manner. But Jasper came to the rescue without being asked.

CHAPTER V

"I SUPPOSE YOU have both been wondering why this planet does not possess the usual polar ice-caps that would be expected on a planet so far from its luminary," he telepathed.

"The reason has to do with our failure to find a suitable world to colonize. I told you that shortly after setting up the cosmic ray projector we were subjected to a long period of intense volcanic activity. This had two effects. Vast quantities of carbon dioxide were released, causing the average temperature of the planet to rise. And the added heat caused prolific vegetable growths, most of them unsuitable for our consumption."

Jasper waxed happily professorial.

"So abundant was the undesirable plant life that it choked out most of the sort of vegetable food we require. As a result, and this in spite of our decreased numbers, there came a shortage of food.

"To beings of our sort, however, this is not really serious, for when we eat less, we merely lessen our bodily activity. And we found it very easy to do this, for the volcanoes caused a thick cloud blanket to cover the planet, nullifying the pulsations of Propus, and removing the necessity for our periodic flying excursions.

"But perhaps the greatest result of the activity was to teach us that we needn't ever multiply to such numbers that the planet cannot hold us. For with the lessened food consumption and lessened activity we found that our division period was lengthened to more than a thousand years.

"And inasmuch as our mental keenness was not impaired by slowing down our bodily activity, it was decided to continue at the new rate, even after food became plentiful."

"How about the sun's pulsations, after the volcanic activity had ceased?" Ham inquired.

"We had learned our lesson," replied Jasper. "And thereafter we took steps to control our climate so that all portions of the planet are ideal for our own existence. It was simply a matter of the amount of suspended dust particles in the atmosphere, and providing means of controlling the proper percentage of carbon dioxide.

"That is why we have no terrifically hot torrid zone, and also no polar ice-caps. The machinery for maintaining this ideal climate is housed in those hemispherical structures you were so curious about, and is completely automatic and self-repairing."

THE SHIP terminated its swift flight in a land of broad plains covered by dense, but stunted, shrubbery. The light of Propus was dim and reddish, coming from such an oblique angle that it lost most of its brightness in the thick blanket of atmosphere through which it passed.

Slim set the ship down a short distance from a structure similar in general appearance to the one they had intended to cut into the day before. This one, Jasper assured them, contained the cosmic ray projector.

It differed from the other buildings in two respects. For one thing, it had a small opening in its lower rim—left there, Jasper told them, so that they could gain entrance to make adjustments in the apparatus.

He explained that while this planet would continue to face its south pole toward the solar system for many ages to come, there was a slow, continual shift taking place, which necessitated correcting the aim of the projector every few millions of years.

The other difference was that the upper portion of the dome was made of a darker colored substance—a better conductor of the rays, they were informed.

Once outside of the ship, Ham strapped one of the lights on Slim's chest, and showed him where to turn on the switch. Slim, in turn, strapped the other on Ham.

There were no blobs of shadow in sight, and they decided that the Mad Ones were temporarily elsewhere. But to warn them of any unexpected attack, Jasper hovered in the air behind them as they headed for the opening in the structure. His brain, keen in telepathic reception, could pick up the jumbled thoughts of the Mad Ones, long before the two men could detect their presence by the sense of sight.

And besides acting as lookout, it was necessary for him to go along to start the machinery of the projector. He had decided against attempting to explain its intricacies, so that they could do it themselves.

But short as the distance to the building was, and clear of menace as the plain seemed to be, there was nevertheless plenty of time for distant Mad Ones to detect their presence and propel themselves to the spot. Like Jasper, they could attain terrific speeds.

The trio had barely gone twenty feet when Slim and Ham were again almost knocked senseless from the intensity of the horror emanations from Jasper's agitated mind.

"Protect yourselves!" he shrilled, the terror thoughts waning and in their stead coming sensations of urgency and desperation.

The two men whirled and darted their eyes all over the landscape, trying to see the shadows that would reveal the Mad Ones. Possibly only a few seconds passed until they saw the inky blobs, hurtling toward them, but those seconds were stretched into minutes by their terrified minds.

But if their brains were temporarily paralyzed by the strength of Jasper's emotions, the condition didn't continue once they had sighted the enemy.

Twin beams of blinding light centered on the nearer of the shadows. When it struck them, clearly outlining their dead-black forms, they seemed to shrivel, hesitate for an instant, and madly plummet to the ground below.

"It works!" Ham exulted. "You're a genius, my boy—albeit a stupid sort of genius." He felt obliged to temper the praise a bit, considering how easily Slim's head was apt to enlarge.

But he had spoken too soon. It became apparent that there

were quite a few of the shadows still in the way, and that some of these had evidently retained enough intelligence to see the danger in the searchlights.

For Ham saw out of the corner of his eye several black streaks fly off to the left of the main body. Divining their purpose, he frantically swerved and caught several of them in the beam from his lamp; but even as he saw them fall, he realized that in the moment that he must hold the beam on them, others were escaping off at a tangent. In a minute they would be coming from all directions.

"Head back for the ship, Slim," he urged. "They're flanking us!"

SLIM NEEDED no coaxing. He had seen those oblique streaks of black and had come to the same conclusion. Grimly the two men strode along, hampered by the necessity of keeping the heavy searchlights continually swerving to catch those of the Mad Ones who were tearing in from the sides.

Sometimes one or the other of them would suddenly whirl and face the rear, warned by some mysterious sense that some of the enemy had managed to circle them.

And each time this occurred they would be rewarded by the sight of one or more of the inky blobs shriveling and dropping. The thought never occurred to them in the heat of the battle, that those warnings could hardly be part of their own sensory equipment. But as it became increasingly apparent that they never could fend off the menacing Mad Ones long enough to reach the safety of the ship, the source of the warnings made itself known.

Unexpectedly, each man felt a constricting band tighten around his waist and abruptly jerk him off his feet. Both thought the same thing—that one of the Mad Ones had finally reached them. They struggled frantically to free themselves, as the unseen being lifted them through the air.

"It is I," came the reassuring tones of Jasper. "Keep the lights working, or they may get us yet."

But in spite of the almost invisible rapidity of their dartings, the searchlights kept the menacing shadows at bay. Several times Jasper was forced to swing one of the men suddenly outward, to let him get a shot at one of the blobs attacking from above; but such was the coordination between amoeba and man, made possible by Jasper's mental equipment, that every attempt by the Mad Ones was frustrated.

Once inside the ship, Slim slumped down at the controls.

"Where do we go from here?"

"We might learn how to build one of those projectors," Ham suggested. "Jasper could give us the dope."

"Where, stupid?"

"Why.... How about Pluto? That's far enough out that a wide-angle projector would cover the rest of the system."

Slim snorted his disgust. "Pluto turns on its axis. How could you keep it aimed?"

Ham pondered this, discarded it; thought up some more ideas, and discarded them too. He was reduced to mentally kicking himself for having voiced a half-baked idea for Slim to scoff at, when suddenly he thought of another, and put it into words without thinking.

"Say!" he exploded. "Suppose we *had* managed to start that contraption. What was there to stop the Mad Ones from turning it off again?"

"Nothing except that I intended to seal the door over after we came out. The Mad Ones are too concerned with the business of finding raw meat to be bothered going to the trouble of breaking in. They weren't after us because we wanted to turn on the projector. All they wanted was a meal."

HAM PACED the floor nervously. Slim continued to slump. Jasper said nothing and did nothing. Ham, glancing at him, decided he looked more like an oversized sofa pillow than an animate being. But then, you could not expect the guy to come out with an idea of how to murder his own relatives.

His glance then strayed idly to the medicine chest. His eyes lighted up avidly. With a quick stride, he reached the cabinet and jerked open the door.

Slim was too far gone in the doldrums even to raise his head at the sound of a familiar gurgle. But he roused himself at the satisfied *aah* which followed.

"Where did you get that?" he wanted to know.

"Medicinal purposes, old chap," explained Ham. "I'm sick. In fact I almost got et. That's enough to make anybody sick."

"I'm sick too," declared Slim, reaching for the bottle.

Fortunately it was only an eight-ounce bottle. If it had been a quart, it would have probably had the unusual effect of putting the pair of them asleep. Jasper, of course, didn't drink.

And if it had been a quart, and they had gone to sleep, then Ham wouldn't have become talkative, and Slim wouldn't have given birth to his prize idea. Such a catastrophe would very likely have changed the course of history on two solar systems.

But, as the chronicle has already recorded, it was an eight-ounce bottle. And Ham did become talkative.

At first he merely marveled that a machine that was potentially capable of operating for millions of years was stilled merely because they couldn't cross a few feet of ground to start it up.

From that his verbal wanderings progressed to wonderment at the methods used to supply power to run the machine all those millions of years. He had completely forgotten Jasper's explanation of that point.

Then he began to reminisce. In the course of which he covered much ground on the subject of power.

"Do you remember," he asked, "back before atomic power was developed?"

"Before my time," Slim grunted, somewhat annoyed.

He was in no mood to be tolerant toward Ham's lapses.

"I'm referring," Ham enlarged, "to the time just before atomic power was harnessed, and shortly after they learned to transmit tight beams of radio power. That was when the Sun Power Company made fortunes for a half-dozen men who had vision. They bought up a vast stretch of jungle land in South America, right on the equator, installed half a million selenium light-gatherers, on poles, and broadcast the power all over the world. Made a fortune selling the receivers.

"But the clever thing about the idea was the way they managed to put power production on a twenty-four hour basis. Broadcasting power from the sun after the sun had set!"

Slim, who had again sunk into a sort of apathy after guzzling his half of the bottle's contents, suddenly snapped to attention, Ham, not noticing, droned on.

"Yeah, that was pretty clever," he repeated. "Hiring two space ships—they were rockets then, too—and having them set up a orbit so that a light-reflecting screen, stretched between them, would send the sun's rays down to make daylight on the night side of the planet. They used to stay there a month at a time, conserving power by dissipating the screen when the sun was shining directly on the Amazon territory."

SLIM, BY this time, was on his feet, striding toward a door which led into the ship's laboratory and work-shop. Jasper, suddenly come to life, floated after him. Ham, a bit bewildered but determined not to show it, followed in their footsteps.

Slim was already at work with a slide rule and a book of logarithms. After a few minutes he stopped, cupped chin in palm, and frowned. Ham was no less bewildered; but Jasper seemed quite aware of what was in Slim's mind. "Power?" he inquired.

"Yes," answered Slim. "It would take more than this ship could produce. I would want a screen a lot bigger than the one those Sun Power lads used."

"Why?" asked Ham, suddenly realizing what they were talking about. "You only need a screen big enough to bathe this particular region, say a mile on all sides, with the full rays of Propus. And while you are up there maintaining the screen, I'll be down here turning on the projector and fusing the doorway shut. Simple, eh?"

"Goofy would be a better word," Slim asserted. "Where would you be while I am going up to erect the screen?"

Ham's face fell. "Et, I suppose," he said, lamely.

But Jasper, who had been indulging in quite a bit of thought along lines foreign to him before meeting these two representatives of a more primitive civilization, decided to take a hand in the discussion.

"Why did you wish to make a screen larger than the one suggested by your friend?" he inquired.

Slim looked steadily at the ameba.

"Jasper, old son, I think you know the answer to that. It was my hope that I could erect a screen, a curved screen, so huge in area that it would bathe the entire night side of this planet with intense sunlight. The thing is possible, too, with enough power. I wanted to exterminate every damned one of those Mad Ones."

"Why, may I ask?" the ameba calmly insisted.

"You may," returned Slim. "Though I think you know the answer to that also. It was because I think you Jaspers are too danged fine a race of beings to be killed off. And that's just what will happen eventually, if the Mad Ones are allowed to continue in existence.

"While your people are living sedate lives, curtailing your rate of division so that the planet will not become over-populated, these creatures are madly thinking of nothing but their carnivorous appetites. And dividing at a terrific pace!

"You have deliberately understated the plight of your people, but I managed to see through your pretense that a reckoning was far in the future. It is imminent!

"Your doom is on top of you. How else could you unconsciously emit such a strong feeling of horror, at the presence of the Mad Ones? At first I thought it was a revulsion at the thought of cannibalism, but the last time it was much too strong to be merely that.

"And yet, in spite of that horror, you forced yourself to stay with us and help us out when the pinch came, even to swinging us around to get a shot at the enemy. Say, old boy, did you realize you were fighting? Well, after the way you acted, even if you had the instincts of a wild boar, I would want to do something for you. That's why I wanted to set up the big screen."

CHAPTER VI

JASPER EVIDENTLY REQUIRED some time to digest all this, for he ventured no comment. Ham, usually voluble, was shocked into temporary silence by the sudden realization that ever since Jasper had explained the nature of the Mad Ones earlier in the day, he had been unconsciously puzzled by hazy, nebulous thoughts about the ultimate fate of the amoebas.

Even then his mind had been toying with the memory of the soul-chilling emanations the amoeba had loosed on the night previous. But it had taken Slim's keen insight to make those thoughts concrete.

"Say, Jasper," Ham finally exploded. "You were saying something about your people never being required to fight any other forms of life in the past. You just rose in the air and fled.

"But just the same your flight was an expression of a universal instinct called self-preservation. And maybe when flight won't do you any good, you'll forget your principles and do what any other form of life does when it's cornered.

"My personal opinion is that you only think you could stand being eaten by a Mad One without trying to fight back. I figure that as individuals you Jaspers will fight when the time conies.

"The only trouble is that when the time comes that you can no longer run, it will be because the Mad Ones have multiplied to the extent that they will begin to pick you off, one at a time, by ganging on you.

"What I'm getting at is that if I'm right, and your people will be forced by the instinct of self-preservation to fight when you are ultimately cornered, why can't you push the calendar ahead a little bit and do your fighting now, collectively while there is still time to save yourselves? You'll do it in the end, anyway, in spite of your finer instincts—but it'll be too late then."

The two men looked at Jasper expectantly but once again he declined to answer.

For a brief moment they fancied there was some mysterious aura surrounding the amoeba. There was an electric tensity in the air that made the silence seem tangible. For a short space they imagined the air shimmered and waved about the figure.

But the impression lasted only an instant, and Jasper became the same inscrutable being he always was. His smooth body was devoid of a revealing feature to indicate the workings of his mind. The incongruous thought passed fleetingly through Ham's mind that the amoeba had the ideal equipment for playing poker. He had something better than a poker face. He had no face at all.

"It'll be too late then," repeated Jasper, absently. "We must find out!"

This made no particular sense to either of the men, nor did Jasper's following actions. He rose slowly from the floor, as if reluctant to continue, and floated toward the airlock. He hesitated over the spot where the men had dropped the powerful searchlights when they had dashed into the ship.

Then abruptly four pseudopodia thrust forth and grasped the two lamps, while a fifth reached out to open the door.

"Remain inside, please," he said, and swung the door inward just far enough to let himself through. It slammed shut before any of the Mad Ones even noticed it had been opened.

AS ONE man, Ham and Slim rushed to the nearest porthole. At first there was nothing to be seen. Jasper was not yet in their range of vision, and the reddish-gray landscape was broken only by an occasional hazy blot, marking the spot where one of the Mad Ones had fallen in the recent skirmish.

Floating in the air were still a few who had not been struck by the light beams; but evidently the majority had moved on in quest of easier prey.

Presently Jasper came in sight as he moved slowly away from the ship; and simultaneously with his appearance two of the hovering Mad Ones plummeted toward him. Twin beams of blinding light met them half-way and down they dropped, seared inwardly by the converted heat from the rays.

Jasper evidently didn't invite further attack, for he retreated toward the ship.

Ham dashed to the door to let him in, then stepped back as Jasper floated slowly past him and deposited the lamps on the floor. Neither he nor Slim spoke when Jasper silently descended to rest beside the searchlights. Both knew that they had witnessed a momentous event.

For Jasper had, without even the driving urge of self-preservation, actually wreaked violence on a living creature. The experience must have shaken him to the core.

"Gentlemen." Jasper finally broke the silence. "My people have come to a decision. I have purposely refrained from telling you this, but ever since your ship entered our atmosphere you have been under observation. And ever since you began to inspect my body, your thoughts have gone forth to all of my race.

"I lied when I said that only when you spoke could I hear your thought vibrations. You would have realized that if you had remembered how long my people have been communicating by this means. The deception was advisable, for if you had known your mind was being probed, you would have been uneasy and suspicious.

"At first we were merely interested in you as two intrepid travelers, exploring a new world. We are great space-people ourselves, and took a kindly interest in you. But before long your thoughts began to stir up something in our placid egos.

"You thought primitive thoughts. Struggle and competition seemed to be the very essence of your existence. Your determination to find a way to restore the decreased rate of metabolism in your people interested us.

"To us, who have lived for millions of years in blissful tranquility, our needs foreseen and provided for without effort, so slothful that we could face our own destruction with equanimity, you—to use your own idiom—started something.

"Possibly it was an eon-long submerged racial vitality coming to the surface; some vital urge dating back before the conscious life of the race; something from the days when our unicelled ancestors struggled in the primal slime of this planet—but your vigorous thoughts of self-perpetuation have stirred a similar urge in us.

"We have come to a decision. We shall throw off this slothful inertia which has gripped us for so long, and destroy the Mad Ones before they destroy us!"

SLIM JUMPED to his feet with a whoop and grabbed the extended hand of a gleeful Ham. Then they turned to Jasper with the full intention of slapping him on the shoulder, but this being obviously impractical, they just stood and grinned.

"But before this decision was made," the amoeba continued, "it was necessary to determine whether or not a Jasper was capable of killing. Your argument that we would do it anyway, after it was too late, had to be tested. It was, therefore, suggested that I try it.

"As I once told you, we are alike in our reactions: if it were possible for me to force myself to do violence, then it would be equally possible for us all to do the necessary thing. And as you saw, I killed.

"You have shown us the way. We shall erect the screen—our mastery of vibration will make it simple—and maintain it until the last of the Mad Ones is dead. We can do this without regret, brothers though they may be, for we know that their state of mentality has fallen below that of the beast.

"Those of the present generation are conscious of but one thing, their appetites. They have no other mental pursuits, so we are fortifying ourselves with the thought that to kill them is no more a crime against our principles than killing the plant life which we use for food.

"We wish to assure you that this is to be accomplished immediately; and as soon as it is done, the cosmic ray projector will be restored to operation.

"Now I must request that you start your homeward journey at once. The thing we are about to do is to us a shameful act, for all its necessity, and we would rather it not be witnessed."

The two earth dwellers, however, saw nothing shameful or degrading about an act of self-preservation; and accordingly, like Lot's wife, looked back. In fact, they did more than look back. They stopped the ship well out of sight of any of the intellectual beings of Propus' second planet, and trained a telescope on it.

Their point of view, it became apparent, was perfect. They had taken off from a point directly at the south-pole of a world of the Jaspers, and were afforded a vision of the complete southern hemisphere. The day side of the planet was a brilliant crescent, vivid in detail, while the night side was a shadowy world.

The Jaspers were as good as their word. After a few minutes of watching it became evident that the work was already begun.

Slim, working frantically at the adjustment knobs on the telescope, brought into focus a vast cloud, its edges wavering and constantly changing, rising from a point on the lighted side of the planet.

Gradually the telescope brought the image closer and defined it more clearly.

Ham gasped as it became apparent that the cloud was composed of millions of Jaspers, rocketing through space at a terrific speed. Neither man had expected anything like this. They had expected to wait several days before anything happened, while the Jaspers constructed machinery to accomplish their purpose.

But obviously these beings were too advanced to require any

such crude methods. They would make the necessary light-reflecting screen by direct manipulation of the energies thrown off by their sun, Propus. Each individual would do his part in constructing the vast reflector.

THE CLOUD approached a point several millions of miles above the dark side of the planet; and as it did the Jaspers which composed it began to diverge, taking paths away from the center of the cloud.

The two men scarcely breathed as they watched the magnificence of the spectacle. Each Jasper was taking his position as if with rehearsed precision. The whole formed a pattern millions of miles across. If lines could have been drawn through the tiny points in the pattern the result would have resembled a circular spider's web of almost unimaginable proportions.

Abruptly the two men slitted their eyes as the vast design flashed into blinding light. Each Jasper, utilizing the accumulated knowledge of a civilization old beyond human conception, was throwing off his portion of that huge mirror.

The darkness below was suddenly turned into blazing day. The reflector was steady, motionless; and the two men knew that it would be maintained that way until every Mad One had given up the ghost.

Swiftly Slim pointed the telescope toward the ground below. But as quickly as he manipulated its controls, even quicker had been the action of the light.

Scattered from pole to equator were evidences that the menace of the Mad Ones was no more. Several times the telescope caught images of animals of varying sizes, dead and partially devoured; and each time they saw the shriveled remains of Mad Ones stricken in the middle of their carnivorous repasts.

At length the two men turned from the telescope and started the ship on its swift journey homeward.

Ham, a few minutes later, was struck with a familiar urge and began to rummage through the supply lockers. He wasn't exactly disappointed when he didn't find any Scotch.

"Some sight, wasn't it?" he remarked.

"Sure was," admitted Slim, bending over a sheaf of charts. "We ought to get a bonus for starting the ball a-rolling."

No answer. Silence, in fact—which was a thoroughly unnatural reaction to the mention of increased emolument. Somewhat alarmed, Slim looked up from the charts. And his alarm was not mitigated by what he saw.

Ham had found a bottle—a pint one, with the amber approximation of one slug of Scotch at the bottom. Yet he had apparently forgotten it; was, in fact, standing rigid, holding the bottle without seeing it. On his face was an expression of deep bereavement.

"For Propus' sake!" Slim exploded. "What's happened now? Who's died? Gimme that—"

Ham shook his head mournfully. "I was just thinking of Jasper. Nicest little gent you'd care to meet on any planet. I guess I'm going to kind of miss him."

"Oh that." Slim started a laugh. "Why he's just—" He paused, nodded. "Yeah," he finished lamely. "Yeah... me too."

And then it came, like a faint music seeping into their minds. Like a memory, distinct but impalpable. "Are my rays strong enough, earth-gentlemen? We are grateful to you, and I personally shall miss you very much."

The two earth-gentlemen stared at each other, nodded slowly in unison. It was the McCoy.

"And now that things are already back to normal on your planet, I have begun to think how pleasant it would be to visit you there. Perhaps, at some future time, it would not be impossible. Meanwhile...."

Ham raised the bottle to his lips, drank exactly half a slug. Bowed profoundly.

And passed the other half-slug over to Slim.

Mother Earth sang happily in her course.

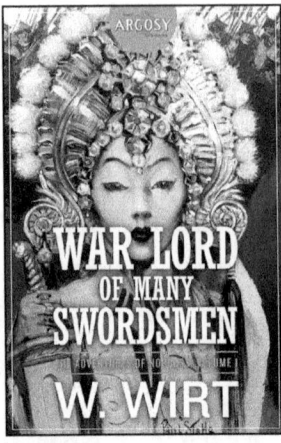